RUSSIAN ROULETTE

David Callan has proved himself a ruthless and effective assassin working for a small section of British intelligence. As a consequence he has made many enemies and very few friends. The Russians have uncovered a British spy inside the KGB but are willing to trade. The price they demand for the mole's safe return is the death of Callan, in revenge for being a thorn in their side. Callan has no say in the matter; he is to be sacrificed. Yet with his eyesight failing and his guns, money and passport all taken from him, Callan has no intention of going quietly.

RUSSIAN ROULETTE

RUSSIAN ROULETTE

by

James Mitchell

Magna Large Print Books
Long Preston, North Yorkshire,
BD23 4ND, England.

British Library Cataloguing in Publication Data.

Mitchell, James
      Russian roulette.

      A catalogue record of this book is
      available from the British Library

      ISBN   978-0-7505-3960-9

First published in Great Britain in 1973

Cover illustration by arrangement with Ostara Publishing

Published in Large Print 2014 by arrangement with
Ostara Publishing

Magna Large Print is an imprint of Library Magna Books Ltd.

Printed and bound in Great Britain by
T.J. (International) Ltd., Cornwall, PL28 8RW

To
GEORGE AND ANNE GREENFIELD

1

The surgeon said, 'Just keep looking into the light,' and Callan kept on looking. It was a kind little light; not like some he had looked at that burned back into your head even when you shut your eyes until somebody hit you and told you to look, to go on looking, to look into the light until you'd answered all the questions.

'Mm,' the surgeon said. Then a little later: 'I see.'

It's all right for you then, thought Callan. But I bloody don't see. That's why I'm here.

The kind little light went out, and the surgeon walked through pools of shadow, tugged at the cords, drew back the heavy curtains. At once the traffic noise intensified, and Callan looked warily at the room: the vast Edwardian desk with its leather top and gleaming brass handles, the heavy, button-back chairs that lived with it so comfortably, and the electric eye-chart that stuck out like a sore thumb. Then the surgeon himself, tall, glittering clean, with the occupational stoop of a man who had spent half a lifetime bending down to look into other people's eyes.

'Well?' the surgeon said.

'It's no good,' said Callan. 'I can still see two of everything.' Two Edwardian desks, two electric eye-charts, two bloody surgeons.

'Of course,' the surgeon said, 'we haven't begun to treat you yet.'

Then treat me for Christ's sake. Treat me before I get hurt.

The surgeon looked at his notes.

'Your doctor says it's of recent origin.'

'Recent – yeah,' said Callan. 'I thought I was drunk at first.'

'Are you a heavy drinker?'

So you don't like jokes, Callan thought. At least you don't like bad ones.

Aloud, he said, 'No ... I'm not.'

'Headaches?' the surgeon asked.

'Sometimes,' said Callan.

'Severe no doubt?'

'Pretty bad.'

'They usually are,' said the surgeon, 'in this kind of condition. Nothing to worry about.'

The headaches don't worry me, Callan thought. I can live with pain better than most. They taught me how to. It's the fear that worries me. Nobody can teach you how to live with the fear.

'We'd better start your treatment,' said the surgeon, and pressed a buzzer.

A voice said, 'Yes sir.' A nice voice, soothing, like a cool hand on an aching forehead.

The surgeon spouted formulae and the voice said, 'Yes sir. At once.'

10

'Drops,' the surgeon said. 'They'll put you right for a while.'

For a while didn't sound so good. The surgeon looked again at his notes.

'You're a book-keeper, I see,' he said.

'That's right,' said Callan.

'Ever play rugby?' Callan shook his head. 'Or soccer? Boxing? No? What I'm trying to establish is whether you've ever indulged in any form of violent exercise, Mr. Callan.'

Callan found that it was possible to want to laugh even when you were looking at two doctors sitting on two chairs behind two desks, like identical twins with exactly equal rights.

'Not much,' he said. Not much— If you didn't count karate, judo, or the section's own brand of unarmed combat, that made the stuff they taught commandos look like a quarrel in a chorus boys' dressing room.

'Have you ever suffered a violent blow?' said the doctor.

Coshes, thought Callan. Karate chops, pistol butts, a number nine boot.

'Not that I can remember,' he said.

And then the girl came in: a rustle of uniform, neatness of movement. Medium height, good legs, figure unobtrusive inside that nurse's get-up. Nothing so blatant as prettiness, but she lit up the room. Her skin was the colour of the doctor's table, and every bit as smooth. For once looking at two

11

of everything had compensations.

'Nurse Somerset will give you your drops,' the surgeon said. 'Just lean back and open your eyes wide. It won't hurt.'

Callan did as he was told. Her hands were as cool and soothing as her voice.

'Were you in the army?' the surgeon asked.

'Yeah,' said Callan. 'A long time ago.'

'Abroad?' said the surgeon.

'Malaya.'

The drop went into his left eye. It was as cold as charity, and as pure.

'Did you see any action?'

'Yeah.'

'Violent action?'

'When you kill people it's always violent,' said Callan.

The girl's hand moved, the drop entered his right eye; an explosion of icy sweetness. He was blind now, totally vulnerable as the drops did their work.

'What I'm trying to establish,' said the surgeon coldly, 'is whether you sustained an injury then that might be affecting your sight now.'

Callan remembered a drunken fight with a sergeant. The sergeant had put the boot in, but even so Callan had half killed him...

'I got kicked in the head once,' he said.

'When?'

'1955,' said Callan.

'That seems rather a long time ago for

such a severe aftereffect,' said the surgeon.

As if it were my fault, thought Callan, then blinked as the mists cleared, to a clouded milkiness, to a haze like a hot day's dawn, to the lights of a room where one surgeon sat in one chair behind one desk.

'Better?' said the surgeon.

'Marvellous,' said Callan.

Nurse Somerset moved from behind his chair, and Callan watched her leave. Now there was only one of her. Any sane man would have found it more than enough.

'It's only a palliative you know,' said the surgeon. 'The retina in both eyes needs attention.'

'An operation?'

'Quite minor. Nothing to be afraid of.'

'How soon?' said Callan.

'The list's rather long,' said the surgeon, and smiled. It was a very human smile, the first hint of the weariness behind the glittering clean façade. 'The best I can do is three weeks from now.'

'Three weeks?'

'I shouldn't delay it. You could lose your sight altogether.'

'And if I have the op?'

'There's an excellent chance. Really excellent,' said the surgeon. Callan knew that special, healer's voice. You couldn't get more out of him with thumbscrews.

'You really will have to face up to it,' the

13

surgeon said. 'In your case this operation is essential. The drops will only work for a month at the most. After that the double vision will increase – and after that–'

'I'll go blind,' said Callan.

'Irrevocably, I'm afraid.'

'I'd better have it then,' said Callan. 'It's just that I was thinking – I'll have to make arrangements, let my boss know.'

'Of course,' said the surgeon. 'But it's not a long operation you know. Your eyes won't be bandaged for more than ten days. You'll be home in three weeks. Surely your – er – boss will be able to manage without you for that long?'

If I lose my sight, thought Callan, Hunter will manage without me for ever.

'He'll just have to, won't he?' said Callan.

'You're very wise,' the surgeon said, and picked up his diary. 'I'll put you down for the sixteenth of next month. You'll get further details in due course.'

Callan stood up.

'Thanks,' he said.

'The effect of those drops will wear off quite soon,' the surgeon said. 'When you need some more, come and see Nurse Somerset. She'll look after you.'

He was reading the notes of his next case before Callan reached the door.

2

Leaving the hospital was bad. The queue for the ambulances looked like a casualty clearing station: maimed men, bandaged women, faces grey with pain, or worry, or both; discharged in the shortest possible time, while Callan put down his money and bought the luxuries of Edwardian desks, private practice, Nurse Somerset's cool fingers. He argued in his mind: But they aren't going to die, and knew even as he thought it that he lied: two at least had that look about them, that look of ultimate surrender. It was good to leave the hospital; walk to the tube, slide down past the half-dressed girls who made underwear look like an orgy, each girl clear in her picture frame because those eye drops worked. For a time.

Callan knew he had to think about that, but he put it off. The tube was no place for thinking: people and judder and noise. The place to think was after you walked through the gates, across what had once been a playground, now littered with half-wrecked cars and vans, and a sign that said: C. Hunter, Ltd. Scrap Metal. That took you to the schooldoors, the television scanners already on you, past the man on duty who didn't even glance as you passed him. His business was to watch the television monitor and he did just that, looking out for uninvited guests, a .38 revolver ready under his arm to make them feel welcome. Anyway, the lookout man would know where Callan was going: down the stairs to what had once been the boiler room and was now the armoury. If there was no flap on, Callan always went to the armoury.

Judd heard the shrill insistence of the buzzer, and looked at the monitor. Callan. Still with that worried look he'd carried for the last few days, but the fingers already working, flexing themselves for suppleness. Judd pressed a button and the armoury's steel doors slid open. Callan stepped into this one familiar world: a room lined with telephone directories, its only furniture a bench littered with guns, its only decoration the targets on the wall facing the guns.

Judd said, 'Come for a work-out, Mr. Callan?'

'That's right,' said Callan.

'What d'you fancy?'

'Magnum 38,' said Callan.

He picked up the gun, and loaded it, and Judd settled back to watch. He was a marksman himself, but this guy was so good it was frightening. But then Callan had to be good

– so long as he wanted to stay alive.

The fingers moved with mindless deftness, and the gun was assembled, loaded, with a precision that made the movements seem slow, even though Judd knew there was no-one in the building who could do it faster, not even himself. Callan stood with his back to the target, then swirled round into a crouch, arm extended, the gun a pointing, accusing finger. There was a series of shots so fast they sounded like one continuous noise, then Judd wound in and looked at the target. The bull was obliterated; the rest of the target unmarked.

'Looks like you've still got it,' said Judd.

But Callan was already reloading.

Aim and fire. Faster, always faster. So fast that the other bloke was always too late, in the half-dark, or in blazing light, crouching, kneeling, prone; with any kind of gun: heavy, light, revolver, automatic. Know them, use them, and live. Hand and reflex and eye. All perfect. Except the eyes now weren't always perfect and Hunter had to be told. 'Sir I'm sorry. My doctor thought I may be going blind and the specialist says he's right, so would it be all right if you didn't ask me to kill anybody for the next few weeks?' With Hunter you never knew. He might decide Callan was too big a risk even if the operation was successful and take him off the active list, send him off to some Ministry of Works fac-

17

tory as Security Officer to find out who was fiddling the tea-money. No more fear, thought Callan. What's wrong with that you bloody fool? Do you want to be afraid? And the answer to that was No I don't. But I don't want to be a Security Officer either... But to tell him, get it over with, endure the inquisition about why he'd gone to a private doctor and specialist, instead of letting Snell have a look at him. Snell, the section psychiatrist, a qualified physician, who'd have whipped Callan over to the best eye-surgeon in Harley Street in the time it took to fire five rounds. The answer was simple. Callan knew the things that Snell had done and hated him so much that he couldn't bear to be touched by him; could look into Snell's eyes only in nightmare. But he'd have to find a better excuse than that to give Hunter.

He moved on to another gun, a target pistol with a four and a half inch barrel, the walnut stock and blue steel gleaming new. Callan picked it up, lifted it. It felt safe and solid in his hand; he liked the wide trigger and ramp front sight.

'Colt Woodsman,' said Judd. 'Target pistol.'

'What kind of ammo?' said Callan.

'22 Long Rifle,' Judd said. 'Want to try it?' He pushed a box of shells across.

As Callan loaded, Judd said, 'Back in the States if you carried one of those you were either bluffing – or you were good.'

Callan looked at the shell in his hand. 'That bullet wouldn't stop much.'

'It's not supposed to be a stopper,' said Judd. 'The Woodsman's made for the man who can shoot, Mr. Callan. The man who can pick his target and hit it. With a shell like that you either hit the guy where it'll kill him or the bullet will go right through him and he won't even know it's happened. I saw a guy in Youngstown, Ohio one time. He stopped three of these – two in the shoulder, one in the leg. And he still walked up to the guy who was firing and brained him with a bottle.'

Callan aimed and fired, taking his time about it. It was a good gun; almost perfect. Where you sighted, the gun sent the bullet, and if you missed it was your fault. You couldn't blame the gun. He fired the ten in the clip and took out the magazine, and as he did so the buzzer shrilled again. Judd looked at the monitor, said, 'Mr. Meres,' and pressed the button that opened the door, as Callan began reloading the clip.

'Sir wants you,' said Meres, and Callan went on reloading. 'Now,' said Meres.

Callan sighed and put down the Woodsman.

'Flap on?' he said.

Meres shrugged. '"Get Callan here," Sir said. To hear is to obey. He is our master after all.'

19

He turned and walked out, and Callan followed. It never paid to keep Hunter waiting. Behind him he heard the soft whoosh of sound as the steel doors of the armoury closed. He looked down at his right hand. In it were three .22 long rifle shells. It was ridiculous for anyone to be as nervous of another human being as he was of Hunter, he thought. But the fact remained that he was. He hurried after Meres and dropped the shells into his pocket. Judd would have to wait for his ammo.

Meres said, 'Shooting well today?'

'Yes,' said Callan.

'Miss at all?'

'No.'

'Not one?'

'Not one,' said Callan.

'You really are awfully good with guns,' said Meres. The thought seemed to amuse him.

'Thanks,' said Callan. 'But what's funny about it?'

'Funny? Nothing,' said Meres, but still laughter lurked in his voice.

Meres, Callan knew, felt only one emotion towards Callan: an unrelenting jealousy so intense it probably invaded his dreams. When he found something Callan said amusing, it was time to get set for the punch.

'What does Hunter want me for?' said Callan.

'I'm just the errand boy, sweetie. I told you,'

said Meres.

'That was for Judd's benefit,' said Callan. 'Now tell me something for mine.'

Meres looked at Callan then: and for the first time Callan could see no hint of jealousy in his eyes.

'Hunter wants to tell you himself,' he said. 'If I were you I'd let him have his way.'

The sign on the door said 'Headmaster' which was about as close as Hunter ever got to a joke. But beyond the door, Callan knew, were a sofa table made by Sheraton, an Aubusson carpet, and a little Renoir oil of a ballet-girl tying her slipper. They were things that had once been in Hunter's own home, and in a sense they still were, thought Callan. The section was his home. He waited as Meres knocked and the calm voice said, 'Come in.' The voice was always calm, just as the man was always calm, no matter what instructions he gave you, no matter who ran the risk of death.

He sat at the sofa-table in his old, expensive, well-pressed suit, as finically neat as ever, the long-nosed, thin-mouthed face both aristocratic and intelligent. He looked what he was, a senior civil servant with a good family background. A planner and decision-maker. Only his planning was the arrangement of executions, the decisions he made were on who should be executed. That was what his section was for; the elimination of undesirables. And they were good at it. Hunter saw to that.

As Meres and Callan entered a girl rose from the table, notebook in hand, neat and impersonal and efficient, and fair, just as Nurse Somerset was neat and impersonal and efficient and dark. And just as memorable.

'That will be all for now, Liz,' said Hunter. 'I'll ring when I want you.'

'Yes sir.'

Liz had that sort of voice too, thought Callan, like a cool hand on an aching head, and she moves well, like Nurse Somerset – and what chance have I got with either of them?

'Sit down, Callan,' said Hunter, and Callan sat. Meres it seemed, had to stand.

'You know I don't like beating about the bush,' Hunter continued, 'and in fact there are some things which can only be said directly or not at all.'

He paused and adjusted a blotting pad so that it lay exactly parallel with the edge of the table.

'I'm afraid you're leaving us, Callan,' he said.

Callan's first thought was: He knows about my eyes.

'You're saying I can resign?' he asked.

'I can understand your surprise,' Hunter

22

said. 'I told you from the beginning that no-one ever resigned from my section. A rule without exceptions.'

'But I'm to be an exception?'

'In a way,' said Hunter. 'Pour yourself a drink.'

Chivas Regal into Waterford crystal: working for Hunter had its compensations...

He still had the bottle and glass in his hand when Hunter spoke again.

'I've done a deal,' he said, in the same calm voice. 'Perhaps the nastiest deal of my career. I'm giving you to the Russians.'

Callan swung round, the bottle and glass in his hands. They'd set him up beautifully. Meres was still standing, his back to the door, but now he held a Walther P38, not quite aimed at Callan. Callan looked at the Chivas Regal bottle in his hand; as an answer to the Walther it was ridiculous. He poured a little more whisky into his glass, and put the bottle down.

'This isn't April Fool's Day, Hunter,' said Callan.

'None of us *are* fools,' Hunter said. 'I mean what I'm saying Callan.'

'For God's sake—' Callan said.

'Please,' said Hunter. 'Let me finish. It's in your own best interests.'

Callan sipped the whisky. 'All right,' he said. 'Tell me what I did wrong.'

'Wrong? My dear David, you haven't made

23

five mistakes since you joined me. You're the best I've got, in fact– That's why the Russians want you.'

'It would seem to me a good reason for you to hang on to me.'

'A very good reason,' said Hunter. 'Almost the best reason. But not quite.'

Callan sipped the whisky again. He needed it now even more than he feared it.

'The KGB picked up our top man in Russia. So far he's alive and unhurt – and he will continue to be so, now that our negotiations are concluded.'

'You're trading me for him?'

'It was like weighing two diamonds,' said Hunter. 'Each perfectly cut, each virtually flawless. Our man in Russia weighed just one carat more. I'm very sorry David.'

'Sorry–'

'I'm incapable of expressing any kind of feeling otherwise than in conventional terms,' said Hunter. 'But I assure you that what I've said is true. I am sorry.'

'You realise what they'll do to me?' said Callan.

'Rather better than you do, I'm afraid.'

Callan put down his glass, and sensed that Meres shifted position slightly. Meres wouldn't fire till Hunter told him, but once the word was given, nothing would stop him.

'You mean they'll interrogate me?'

'Of course not,' said Hunter. 'If all they

wanted was information, they would ask me for it direct.'

'A show trial?'

'You've already been tried, David, and sentenced.'

'Tried for what – for God's sake?'

Hunter ticked them off on his fingers.

'The killing of Karski, the killing of Lebichev, the exposure of Tania Andreyevna, the Bokharin scandal, Kliegmann's suicide – shall I go on?'

'But those were jobs,' said Callan. 'Jobs you set up–'

'And you carried out. Successfully. All too successfully for them.'

'Spell it out,' said Callan.

'They want you dead,' said Hunter. 'They want it so badly that they're prepared to give me my top man back unharmed, in exchange for you.'

'For my corpse.'

Hunter said, 'They would get it anyway. I have their word on that.'

'*Their* word–'

'This time they would keep it. I'm quite sure of that. If I didn't agree to the exchange, they were determined to kill you anyway – and keep my man into the bargain. *I* had their word on that too. It would take half the resources of this section just to keep you alive – if the KGB mounted a most urgent operation against you. You're worth a great deal to me, David, but not half the section, plus the best agent I ever had in Russia. I'm telling you to go.'

Callan looked across at Meres, who was examining the Walther as a show-girl might examine a new necklace.

'Won't this be bad for morale?' he asked. 'If the word gets around that you don't mind killing off the rank and file–'

'The word won't get around.'

'Meres knows.'

'Meres dislikes you,' said Hunter. 'He also wants your job. And he'll get it. He has no reason to tell the others.'

'Is he the one who's going to kill me?'

'I could not agree to anyone in this Section killing you,' said Hunter. 'I told the KGB so.'

'Did you tell them why?'

'Of course,' said Hunter. 'I found that I just couldn't issue such an order.'

'That must have been a shock to them.'

'On the contrary. They quite appreciated my reluctance. If anything I think they mean to turn it to account. They intend to kill you themselves, David. In that way it will seem more like an execution.'

'You're going to let them come in here and set up a firing squad?'

Hunter said, 'Do try to listen. I told you you were leaving us – and you are. You're going back into the world, David. Beyond

26

my protection.'

'And they'll just walk in and kill me?'

'I know nothing of the *modus operandi*,' said Hunter. 'I assume it will be efficient.'

'You think they'll be able to find me then?'

'Of course,' said Hunter. 'I've told them where to look.'

Callan felt his whole body react to that one.

'Christ,' he said. 'You're a cold-blooded bastard.'

'If I weren't,' said Hunter, 'I'd be incapable of doing this job.'

'How many are they sending?' Callan asked.

'Three,' said Hunter. 'The very best they have. You will have no chance at all.'

'I could run,' said Callan.

'No,' said Hunter. 'You couldn't. You won't be able to leave the country. We'll see to that.'

'I'll fight them,' said Callan. 'You know I'll fight them. I won't die easy.'

'You have no chance,' Hunter said. 'You have no gun, and no way of getting one.'

'It would save a lot of time and trouble if I just killed myself.'

'It probably would,' said Hunter.

'Might annoy the Russians though,' said Callan. 'They want to do the job for me.'

'Oh I think they'd find suicide acceptable,' Hunter said. 'The fact that you killed yourself

27

rather than face their executioners would be very good for morale.' He looked at Callan's glass. 'Won't you finish your drink?'

'Why not?' said Callan. 'It'll be the last one.'

'I'm afraid it will,' said Hunter. 'Perhaps you'll just let Meres search you while you're doing it.'

'I'm not carrying a gun,' said Callan.

'Indeed you're not,' said Hunter. 'But there are other things.'

'I don't use them.'

'It's my business to see you have no chance to.'

'Up,' said Meres. 'Don't try anything.'

Callan thought: What can I try? If I start something now Meres will belt me, and if he belts me on the head I'll go blind, and the KGB will kill me in the dark.

He stood up and waited, passive, as Meres' hands explored his body in the impersonal degradation of a skilled search.

At last Meres said, 'Nothing sir.' Then he looked at Callan and laughed. 'I never thought you'd give so little trouble,' he said.

'Perhaps he's conserving his energies,' said Hunter. 'Are you Callan?'

'Can I go?' Callan asked.

'In a moment. You're on good terms with Judd in the armoury I believe.'

'We shoot together,' said Callan. 'I mean we used to.'

'You're aware of his background?'

'He carried a gun for a mob in Youngs-town, Ohio.'

'The only Englishman ever to do so. He likes you Callan – but he's afraid of me. To the Judds of this world, fear is a far more potent influence than friendship. Don't try to get a gun from him, Callan. Don't even try to speak to him – or anyone else in this section. You won't succeed.'

'You know,' said Callan, 'I never expected to get a pension out of this job – or even a gold watch. But I never thought I'd be fired, either.'

'There's no animosity in my decision,' said Hunter. 'I thought you'd realised that.'

'Oh I realised it,' said Callan. 'But there's animosity in mine. If I come through this I'm going to kill you, Hunter.' He looked at Meres. 'And you.'

He walked out then, and for the first time in his life he slammed the door.

Hunter looked at Meres. He still held the Walther as if it were an extension of his hand.

'Put that thing away,' said Hunter.

Meres looked at the gun, almost in sur-prise, and put it back into the harness under his arm.

'You should have let me do it, sir,' he said.

'No,' said Hunter.

'But sir I–'

'You wanted to do it, Toby,' Hunter said. 'Over-eagerness might make you vulnerable and I can't have you damaged now that I've lost Callan.' He looked at Meres more closely, as if he were seeing him for the first time. 'I need you now more than ever,' he said. 'God help me.'

3

Adrenalin carried him out of the Section, down a twist of streets to a bus that he hopped on to, careless, unthinking, like a man with no eye-sight to lose. The cold-blooded bastard to do a thing like that. And bloody Toby Meres sitting there. He couldn't stop laughing he was so happy. He'd kill them. Once this was over he– That was when the thought hit him. Once this was over he'd be dead. In the old days when you were done for murder the judge used to put a bit of black silk on top of his head and go into a long rigmarole about taking you back from whence you came and there or in some other place to be appointed you shall be hanged by the neck until you were dead.

He'd known a feller in the Scrubs who'd heard those words: a little Welshman who'd killed a tart, then got a reprieve. Used to go on about them all the time. And the way he felt. Half the time you didn't believe it, but the other half you did. You knew they were going to do it – to you – and you felt cold. You didn't shiver, but you felt frozen, right through to your bones. Like he felt frozen now, after the whisky had died on him and there was no adrenalin left.

He wanted to go back to his own place, and that was barmy. Hunter could put a tail on him there if he hadn't got one on him already. Bloody stupid idiot Callan tearing off in righteous rage and not even looking to see if he was being followed or not. All right then. Don't go back to the flat. See if they're tailing you now and make a break for it. Disappear. Except that you need money – and a gun if you've got one hidden, and all the money he'd got was in the flat, and so was the gun, and if those bastards were coming for him he wanted a gun in his hand no matter what risks he had to take. Eyesight or no eyesight, if he got the gun he wouldn't die easy.

The West Indian bus-conductor said, 'You all right man?'

Callan looked up at him; thin, tired, wary, but there was pity in the face, and maybe a little pleasure in the realisation that Whitey has troubles too.

'I'm fine,' Callan said. 'Why?'

'Because I just asked you three times for your fare.'

'Sorry,' said Callan. 'I was thinking. Oxford Street please.'

The conductor twirled his ticket machine.

'The way I look at things a man can do too much thinking,' he said. 'If it going to happen it going to happen. Isn't nothing you can do about it.'

In the army they used to say that the bullet that had your number on it would find you. It was the same thing. Only nobody ever believed that there was one with his number on it. There had to be some chance, and if there wasn't, you had to make one.

He sat on as the bus ground its way across the East End – dingy stone, ageing brick, and dotted between them the tall shafts of high-rise council flats. People-packing. Just what he needed. A room in the middle of one of them, with humanity all around you like a wall... Except that people nowadays were trained to believe that it was wrong to get involved. You could scream your bloody head off and all they would do would be to turn up the volume on the telly... He waited as the bus moved through Bethnal Green and Hoxton, and by that time he knew that everybody on the lower deck, where he sat, had come on after him. Watch the lights now. There was a tube station just down the road, just by the lights. If they were on red, he'd make his move.

The lights changed to amber as the bus hammered down like the spear-head of a panzer division, but the driver saw a police-car in his mirror and decided that he'd better not risk it. As his foot touched the brakes Callan was already moving, in a frantic leap to get off, a scurry across the line of waiting traffic to reach the steps down to the tube, that burrow which is every rabbit's friend. As he raced down he heard the conductor yell from the platform, 'You got the wrong stop, thinking man,' but he hurried on anyway, fed coins into a machine, and raced towards the thunder of an approaching train.

It took him another hour to reach his flat, but when he did so he knew that no-one was following him. The thought cheered him a little, but not much. They might be waiting for him there already. The hardest part of the exercise would be to get inside. He walked down the road, across the street from the block that contained the flat where he lived. Nobody hanging about, but there wouldn't be. Only amateurs hang about. Callan walked on further to a newsagent's, and bought a girly-magazine; full colour, expensive paper, page after page of pampered flesh. He had never in his life felt less need to look at flesh, but if you folded it right it made a formidable weapon. If you moved quick enough, you could cut a man's throat. Callan folded it right and crossed the street, thinking, three of them. Executives. The best in the business. And each one with a Makarov semi-automatic they'll have trained with for years. And what have I got? A Penthouse Pet.

To cross the hall and climb the stairs took almost all the courage he had left, but after that there was still a landing to be crossed and a door to be opened before he could

34

face whatever lay beyond. He stood in the shadows, took out his key in his left hand and crossed towards his door, holding the girly-mag like a weapon. His key had almost reached the lock when the door behind him opened and he spun round, the girly mag lifting in his hands, to face his neighbour, Miss Brewis, in her best tweed coat and real leather handbag, ready for an evening's bridge.

'You're late tonight, Mr. Callan,' she said.

'Yes,' said Callan. 'I – got held up.'

Her eyes were fixed to the magazine, and did not like what they saw.

Two men from the Gas Board came to see you this afternoon,' she said. 'There was some talk of a leak or something. Some man from the landlord's office let them in.'

'Gas Board?' said Callan.

'It was perfectly in order,' Miss Brewis said. 'The man from the landlord was with them – and I kept an eye on them from time to time. They didn't steal anything, I'm sure.'

'You're very kind,' said Callan.

'The least I could do,' said Miss Brewis, but her eyes were still on the magazine. She wouldn't do it again.

'They seemed quite satisfied that every-thing was in order when they left,' she said.

'So I won't blow myself up when I make a cup of tea,' said Callan.

'I don't think any of us are liable to do

that,' Miss Brewis said, and looked at her watch. 'I must be off. Goodnight, Mr. Callan. Enjoy your reading.'

Her feet rat-tatted angrily down the stairs, and Callan let the magazine uncurl in his fingers, made no attempt at silence as he put the key in the lock. Even Miss Brewis wanted to get rid of him now, it seemed. But at least if she'd been watching he could be sure no-one was hidden in the flat.

It wasn't a marvellous flat, but it suited him. Space to cook, space to bathe, and space for his model soldiers and books – volume after volume of military history. Even space for his war-games, if he pushed all the rest of the furniture to the walls. The flat had all he wanted – including the most burglar-proof locks in the business. Locks he'd made himself when he first moved in, using skills he'd been taught when he'd been apprenticed to Bartram's locksmiths twenty years before, the craftsman's skills, once learned, that never leave your hands. No bloke from the landlord's office had opened his door, but whoever had opened it had done a marvellous job. The lock wasn't even damaged.

He went from living-room to bathroom to bedroom to kitchen. Everything looked just as it had when he'd left it, except for the gas-cooker. They'd put a new burner on one of the rings. Nice touch that. Elegant. He put

36

the chain on his front door and went back to the living-room. He knew beyond doubt what he was going to find, but he had to do it anyway; had to be sure that his last hope was destroyed. He pulled back the carpet, and looked at the boards beneath. Two of them had screws instead of nails. He looked and saw that the screws were still there, turned tight as he had left them. He fetched a screw-driver and unscrewed them, lifted out the boards. In the cavity below was a box of heavy metal. Callan took it out, tried the latch and found that it was locked, as it should have been. His hand was shaking as he took out the key, put it in the lock, turned it, lifted the lid. The box had two compartments, one for a passport with another name, and a thousand pounds in dollars, Swiss francs, sterling; the other for a magnum .38 revolver and twenty rounds of ammunition. Both compartments were empty.

Oh the bastards. The neat, tidy, sadistic bastards. To offer him hope right to the very end, and then knock him down like that. He could have borne it better if they'd wrecked the place. Wearily Callan screwed back the floor-boards, pulled the carpet straight. When the phone rang he knew at once who it would be.

'Callan,' he said.

Liz said, 'Hold on please. Charlie wants to speak to you.'

The drill, always the drill; even after they'd sentenced you to death.

'Wasn't it a little unwise to go to your own address?' said Hunter.

Callan said, 'I had some things to collect – or I thought I did.'

'We collected them for you,' said Hunter.

'Yes. So I've just found out.'

'No passport, no gun, no money.'

Callan said nothing.

'You're thinking of your bank account,' said Hunter. 'Did you think I'd forgotten it?'

'No,' said Callan. 'Just wondering how you stole it.'

'I've brought an action for bankruptcy against you,' Hunter said. 'All your assets are frozen, old chap – including your four hundred and thirty two pounds in the current account.'

'So I'll die broke,' said Callan.

Hunter waited a moment, then said, 'Your gas supply is still working, I think you'll find.'

'Forget it, Hunter,' Callan said. 'Whoever's going to do their killing for them – it won't be me.'

'You won't believe it,' said Hunter, 'but the advice was well meant.'

'You're telling me you're sorry?'

There was a pause.

'I may be one day,' said Hunter, and hung up.

There was no time to think about that. The implications of Hunter's words reached out to a future that Callan wasn't going to have, unless he could turn his mind to the here and now. The time for his death was fixed; any day now. Maybe the undertaker had started work already, and the best he could do was run... He looked round for whisky and brewed coffee instead, black and treacle-sweet, and sipped it as he examined his assets. Assets... The word was a joke. Two goodish suits, a raincoat, three pairs of shoes, a hand-made shirt bought after a job in Madrid, and that was about it. No gold cuff-links, no little bit of Meissen or jade... Just some clothes he could pawn for a fiver – and the soldiers. Idiot, he'd forgotten the soldiers.

He went to the war-game table and looked at the ones laid out. The Battle of Talavera – July, 1811. He'd made that stuff himself in thirty millimetre, and it looked what it was – durable but rough. But the fifty-four milli-metre solids he'd bought – then painted up himself; they were something else again. A section of a British square at Waterloo; the four ranks standing up to a charge of French cuirassiers; it looked like a three-dimensional battle painting of the kind he'd loved as a kid; the kind of picture that had got him hooked on the whole war-game business in the first place: gallant officers, grizzled veterans, ner-vous boys seeing their first action: every detail painted exactly as it had been one hundred and fifty-eight years ago: the weapons right, the uniforms right, even the faces right: the huddled mixture of shock, rage, fear and agony as they faced the giant horsemen and refused to run... There's a lesson for you there, Callan, he thought. But there wasn't, not really. These men hadn't run because their mates hadn't run and the hedge of bayonets they erected was too much for even the finest horsemen in Europe. But the point was they had mates... And he'd got them right, too, the gleam of armour, the intricacy of the horses' trappings, and on the riders' faces the onset of despair. Good work, the work of a craftsman, done with skill, and pride in achievement. Worth five hundred quid of anybody's money, and plenty of collectors daft enough to pay it. He must have been rattled to have forgotten the soldiers.

Callan went to the mahogany box he'd made for them with the same skill and pride – velvet lined, counter-sunk lid, polished, rubbed down, polished again. The best of his life really; the one talent he had that could actually make something instead of destroying... He opened the box to find that Hunter hadn't forgotten either. The neatly lined shelves were empty, every one, and all the money he had was twenty-three quid in notes – and a few new pence. He turned out his pockets: pen knife, keys, thirty-one new

pence – and three Long Rifle .22 calibre
bullets and no bloody gun to put them in. He
went back to the kitchen then, and looked at
the gas-stove. It would be easy enough. The
windows fitted tight. Put a cushion inside the
oven so you could lie comfortably, finish off
the whisky as death built up inside you– Easy.
Dead easy. If he couldn't find a gun.

4

Getting out of his flat was as bad as getting in. There was no way of telling who was watching, who was waiting. He broke into Miss Brewis's and went through her skylight on to the roof, then down by the non-conformist chapel where the junkies slept. 'Jesus lives', said the torn and flapping poster outside, and underneath someone had written: 'You call this living?' Somebody who hadn't yet had to face the ultimate decision: whether or not mere survival was good enough to settle for.

The night was cold, and he was bone weary. Buses, tube-stations, glowed their invitation, but twenty-three pounds thirty-one pence was all he had in the world: he couldn't afford to waste it on public transport. What he needed was a car. He could steal one – no trouble – the section had taught him how, but Callan had hated stealing ever since they let him out of the nick. Maybe he'd have to do it, sooner or later, but he wasn't ready for it yet, like he wasn't ready for the gas-oven. It was better to walk, and test out if you were being followed or not, never quite relaxing, because even though you couldn't see or hear anybody you could never quite be sure; not with the ones who'd been sent to put you away. They were good like you were good – and there were three of them.

Three mates. And Callan didn't have a friend in the world, except one. A nervous little friend, with a problem that all the deodorants in the world couldn't cure. When he was frightened, he stank, and he was frightened most of the time. They called him Lonely, and no wonder; it was like going mates with a sewage-farm. And yet, Callan thought as he slogged on, there'd been value in their friendship, just as there had been value in making those model soldiers... They'd met in the nick after Callan had done his first and only job. Burglarious entry. Attempted larceny. Twenty-five thousand pounds. A stupid job done for no reason except that his bird had left him and he was bored after Malaya because he was an oddball, a nut-case; the only man in his unit who actually missed the excitement and the dangers of Malaya. The only one who missed the killing; the risk of being killed. Crazy, he must have been. So he'd done the supermarket to see if there was any excitement in that – and there wasn't. It was as easy as catching a bus. Walk in and open it up and help yourself. To anybody trained by Bartram's it didn't even mean working up a sweat. Not till the night-watchman found him... Skinny old gaffer who should have been tucked up in bed trying to out-snore his missus, not creeping around a draughty supermarket hanging on to a young tearaway just out of the commandos, who could have broken his neck as easy as breaking a ruler– And didn't, because the night-watchman still wasn't the excitement he was looking for. The old sod had yelled blue murder and Callan had run for it – straight into a crowd of coppers. He got two years.

He spent some of it with Lonely, who'd been done for housebreaking: money and goods value fifty pounds, with seventeen similar offences taken into consideration, against Callan's twenty-five thousand quid. By prison standards that made Callan five hundred times the man Lonely was... They were three in a cell because two was immoral. That was a laugh for a start. The antics some of those threes got up to would make a monkey blush. But anyway their three didn't try anything: you couldn't work up much feeling for romance over Lonely and their fellow cell-mate, a loony arsonist who specialised in churches. Not that he'd ever been bent anyway – and he was still browned off about his girl letting him down. He'd had a hard enough time in prison without the sex.

Lonely became a mate because he was there, and there wasn't much future in talking to the loony, who spent his waking life either reading the bible or preaching sermons; but Lonely you could at least talk to – once you'd persuaded the loony to belt up. And in the end even the sermons didn't bother them, they talked right through them as if they were a programme on the telly they didn't want to watch; didn't even hear them half the time. But he heard Lonely, and learned the miseries of the petty crook's life when the petty crook is small and frightened and the whole world about him threatening and big.

Lonely was that kind of petty crook, descended from a long line of petty crooks; every single member of his family was bent. Pickpockets, shoplifters, prostitutes; somehow they could see no point in anything else. Trying to explain honesty to Lonely was like extolling a pop group to a deaf man. There was no way you could connect... But he knew all about prisons, and he was willing to share his knowledge. If he hadn't, Callan would have had an even rougher ride than he did, when he'd won a fight with some geezers trying to form a tobacco syndicate, and the warders had worked him over for disturbing the peace. The nick was like that: great stretches of boredom interspersed with violent irrationality.

But Lonely helped him after the warders' beating – the loony had preached right through the whole thing: Saint Paul to the Corinthians, Chapter 13 Verse 1: Though I speak with the tongues of men and of angels, and have not charity, I am become as sounding brass or a tinkling cymbal...

Lonely had lain facing the wall and covered up his ears; but afterwards he'd bathed Callan's bruises and taught him how to stay out of trouble... Lonely was all right, but Jesus, he smelled when he was frightened. Screws were always sending him to the baths, but fright doesn't wash off that easy. When Callan's bruises healed and he could look out for Lonely, Lonely stopped smelling. It was as simple as that: until Callan was due for release. After that he smelled worse than ever, worrying about some geezer called Rinty who Lonely said was going to carve him when he got out. So Callan had gone to see Rinty, and after a while had persuaded him to see reason, and Lonely had come out of the Scrubs unmarked... He'd owed Callan a favour for that one, and paid it back long ago, but there'd been other favours since: favours he wouldn't deny; not least because he was terrified of Callan, and the things he was capable of doing. If anybody could get Callan a gun, Lonely could – if he could find him.

His gaff the last Callan had heard was Notting Hill way, but he wouldn't be in it till the

46

pubs were shut – not if he had any money. And Lonely could usually find money for beer – under the mattress or in the sugar jar or behind the pants in the chest of drawers: whatever dim place the housewife thought the burglar wouldn't ever dream of looking as she slammed the front door and left the back window open. Lonely would have money and the pubs would have beer, so Callan knew he'd have to wait, and it wasn't getting any warmer. He walked straight up to the decaying lump of brick and stucco where Lonely had the top flat. The street was empty, and he could sense no movement in the shadows as he climbed the stairs. Once the place had been occupied by some geezer of what they called modest affluence: a wholesale grocer or a solicitor maybe, with three or four underpaid maidservants humping coal up the back stairs so he could warm his trouser-seat in front of the fire and tell his wife what a grand place Old England was for people who weren't afraid of work; but now the house was on its uppers, as if the grocer or solicitor was hooked on meths and watching himself go to hell as he drank it.

Every room in the place was let off: the alterations done with hardboard nobody had time to paint. Tellys blared from one room after another, drowning the soft creak of Callan's feet on the bare, decaying stairs. He passed landing after landing, the points of danger, and heard nothing more frightening than a good cowboy shooting a bad cowboy in that manly, regretful way good cowboys have, until at last he arrived at Lonely's pad; the eagle's nest, thought Callan. The bloody penthouse. No telly blaring here; not even a bloody light showing. He tried the door handle, but the place was locked up tight. When he knocked there was no answer, and he hadn't expected one. All the same it wouldn't do to hang about.

He took the bunch of keys from his pocket; keys he'd made himself. The first one he tried opened the door in eight seconds; probably faster than Lonely could do it with the key the landlord provided. He let the door swing open, slipping off his raincoat as he did so. Nobody shouted, nobody even breathed. Callan counted to three, then threw the coat into the room. It landed with a soft thud, and Callan moved in as it fell, waiting for the champagne cork popping of silenced guns. Still nothing, and his hand, light as a moth, moved up the wall and pressed the switch... Across an empty room Callan looked at himself in a mirror, and noted without surprise that he was sweating, then shut the door and examined the room.

That Lonely had the acquisitiveness of a jackdaw Callan knew perfectly well, but even he wasn't prepared for what he saw. The grimy gas-stove and sink were fixtures and fittings, standard for every room in the place, but the rest of it reflected the uniqueness of Lonely's personality in a way that only possessions can. Three tellys, none of them with plugs, a brass cannon of the kind used for starting yacht-races, a complete set of Encyclopaedia Britannica, brand new, upside down on a shelf, and a four-poster bed with rotting curtains and a mattress that looked as if a platoon of infantry had slept on it in full equipment. Pictures from girly mags were pasted to the walls, but over the mantelpiece, the place of honour, was the Annigoni portrait of the Queen, flanked by the Royal Arms, and on the mantelpiece itself more soaps, deodorants, bath-salts, than Callan ever knew existed, and well-thumbed books on self-improvement, on how to increase your word-power, on acquiring a more positive personality, on making friends and influencing people. It was all Lonely; frightened, stinking, totally aware of his defects, always meaning to do something about them, never quite getting round to it – and never bloody there when he was wanted. Callan switched off the light, lay down on the four-poster and prepared to wait. Once you'd done a stretch you developed a talent for waiting.

Even from outside the door, Callan could

smell the fish and chips, a smell that reminded him that he was hungry. He waited, silent, as Lonely came in, shut the door, switched on the light.

'I hope you brought enough for two,' he said.

Suddenly the room smelled of rather more than fish and chips, and Lonely shot up as if Callan had rammed a needle into him.

'Mr. Callan,' he said at last. 'You didn't half give me a turn.'

Callan sniffed. 'So I noticed,' he said. He swung his feet from the bed. 'Shall I get the plates?'

'It's me supper,' said Lonely.

Callan shook his head. 'Our supper,' he said.

Lonely sighed, and opened a cupboard. It was stacked with enough china to stock a restaurant.

'How did you get in here, Mr. Callan?' he asked.

'I've got my methods,' said Callan. 'You're getting careless, old son– One of these days you might have burglars.'

'Nothing much here worth thieving,' Lonely said. 'It's what you might call sentimental value mostly.'

'Or the coppers might walk in,' said Callan.

'Bought it all at jumble sales,' said Lonely. 'They couldn't prove any different.'

Callan looked at the battered four-poster.

'That?' he said. 'At a jumble sale?'

'That's legitimate that is,' Lonely said. 'Bought and paid for.'

'I believe you,' said Callan. 'You'd look a right nana with that under your coat.'

He looked at the plates Lonely had set out. Nice pieces. Wedgwood. And a pair of nice pewter mugs off somebody's mantel-piece. Modern, but nice.

'You have been busy,' he said.

'Doesn't pay to be idle, Mr. Callan,' said Lonely, and shared out the fish and chips, poured out bottled beer. Callan sat facing him, and Lonely raised his tankard. 'Old Comrades Association,' he said.

'You what?' said Callan.

'To those who can't be with us tonight,' said Lonely. 'On account of being inside.'

Callan raised his tankard, then watched as Lonely shook the sauce-bottle over his chips.

'But you've got vinegar on them,' he said.

'Course I have,' said Lonely. 'Vinegar's free.'

I suppose you think you've explained yourself, thought Callan, and helped Lonely to eat his supper.

While the food lasted, Lonely was cheerful enough, and talked about the Loony and Rinty, and the wall-eyed git of a screw who'd belt you one with his keys if you didn't slop out fast enough. Just a couple of old school chums, remembering the dear old alma mater. But once he'd got some scoff down his throat the brain started turning at last. Blimey, you could almost hear the cog-wheels creaking, thought Callan.

'What can I do for you, Mr. Callan?' he said.

'You think I've come for something?'

Lonely's hand shook as he reached for his tankard, but he fought the fear, and won for once. When he spoke it was almost with dignity.

'I don't see much of you when things is all right,' Lonely said.

'Maybe. But I've helped you in the past. Now haven't I?'

'I don't deny it,' said Lonely. 'You've been a good friend to me – in the past.'

'That's right,' said Callan. 'Now I want you to be a good friend to me.'

The smell came then; real, vintage Lonely.

'I can't do your sort of jobs,' said Lonely, and Callan willed himself to sit still.

'And what sort of jobs would they be?' he asked.

Lonely looked bewildered. 'The heavy stuff,' he said. 'Like what you done bird for. Like the way you was in the nick. Fighting and duffing blokes and that. I'm no good at it Mr. Callan. Believe me I'm not.'

'I believe you,' said Callan. 'Anyway, I'll do my own fighting, old son. I always have.'

Slowly the air began to clear.

'What is it then, Mr. Callan?'

'I'll tell you,' said Callan; then found it wasn't going to be as easy as he thought. How does an emperor tell a peasant he's in need of a hand-out? He took refuge in a savage pedantry that left the little man more bewildered than ever.

'I find myself at a pecuniary disadvantage,' he said.

'Beg pardon?'

'I'm financially embarrassed,' said Callan. 'Of course I need hardly say it's purely temporary.'

'Come again, Mr. Callan?'

'Put it this way,' said Callan. 'I'm skint.'

Lonely looked at the expensive suit, the hand-made shirt; then down to Callan's hands; broad, capable, utterly relaxed; looked at last into Callan's eyes, eyes he remembered, that told a geezer nothing, even when he was giving the geezer the belting of a lifetime.

'You?' he said. 'You're joking.'

'I wish I was,' said Callan.

The bewilderment faded at last, to be replaced by pity – and by something else he'd seen that day. Then Callan remembered the West Indian bus-conductor. Behind the pity, trying to hide it so it wouldn't show, was Lonely's pleasure in realising that even Mr. Callan had his troubles; that he too was but mortal.

'I've got a bit put by,' said Lonely. 'For a rainy day like. It isn't much but you're welcome.'

'Thanks,' said Callan. 'Thanks, old son.'

'I can let you have – fifty,' said Lonely. Callan gave no answer.

'I mean seventy-five,' said Lonely. Still no answer.

The little man said in desperation, 'Mr. Callan – a hundred's all I've got.'

'I hate to do this to you,' said Callan. 'But it's a bit of an emergency you see.'

'You haven't lost it have you?' Lonely asked, and at once Callan thought of his eyes.

'Lost what?' he said.

'The hard bit,' said Lonely.

'No,' said Callan. 'That's one thing I haven't lost. Not yet.'

'That's all right then,' said Lonely. 'I was afraid someone might be after you.'

Once more Callan was silent.

'Of course if you don't want to tell me–' said Lonely.

'There's nothing to tell,' said Callan. 'Except I'm broke, and I'm asking a mate for some help.'

'I've offered,' said Lonely. 'You can't say I didn't. Just tell me how much you want.'

'How much are guns these days?' said Callan, and again there was the smell. 'For God's sake,' Callan said. 'There's no need to stink the place out just because I asked a question.'

'You really want one?'

'Of course I want one,' said Callan.

'If I got it for you – they could do me for aiding and abetting.'

'And I could do you for not aiding and abetting,' said Callan. 'Only I haven't. I'm asking. Because I thought you were a mate.'

'I'll get you a gun,' said Lonely.

'Magnum revolver .38 if you can manage it,' Callan said.

'I'll do me best, Mr. Callan,' Lonely said, and looked at the clock on the sideboard – a Disney alarm, with Donald Duck instead of the figure six, head nodding like a lunatic.

'You expecting someone?' Callan asked.

'If you don't mind, Mr. Callan,' Lonely said. 'It might be a bit embarrassing if he sees somebody else here.'

'If who sees?'

'This bloke I'm working with.'

'You got a job on?'

'Out Highgate way,' said Lonely. 'It's a bit far – but this bloke's got the loan of a van.'

He broke off as Callan erupted to his feet, lifted him bodily from his chair.

'You great steaming nit,' said Callan. 'You're supposed to be getting me a gun.'

'I will get you one,' Lonely said. 'Honest I will.'

'Suppose you get nicked?' said Callan.

Lonely looked down at the hands holding his collar, hands that he knew could smack him senseless in seconds – hands he'd seen do just that. He licked his lips, but there was no saliva on his tongue. His fear was evident to both of them. At last he said: 'Guns cost money, Mr. Callan. I got to earn it,' and Callan let him go.

'Aah,' he said. 'I'm sorry old son. I'm a bit jumpy.'

'That's all right,' Lonely said. 'I'll get the gun for you tomorrow.'

'Thanks,' said Callan.

'Bring it to your place?'

'My place? I don't have a place any more,' said Callan. 'I was hoping you'd let me kip here.'

'Mr. Callan, I can't,' said Lonely. 'Not when I got this geezer coming.'

'No,' said Callan. 'I suppose not.' He picked up his coat. 'I'd better be off then.'

'Isn't there anybody you can go to?' Lonely asked.

'I'll find a place,' said Callan, and the relief on Lonely's face was immediate.

'Where'll I come for the gun?' Callan asked. 'Here?'

'I wouldn't want to risk a shooter here,' said Lonely. 'Make it me aunty's place.'

Callan had never known anyone with more relatives than Lonely. He must have had thirty aunts at least.

'Which one?' he asked.

'Gertie,' Lonely said. 'The one with the

coffee-stall in the market. She might be able to lend me a few quid for you an' all.'

'I'll pay it back,' said Callan.

'Course you will,' said Lonely. 'I only wish you didn't need a gun to do it.'

Then Callan had to start walking again. Getting late now; time respectable people were in bed. Soon the coppers would start looking at him if he wandered about like this; or a Panda car would pull up and the questions would start. 'Lost your way have you sir?' And a good sniff at his breath to see if he was drunk. And anyway, he didn't dare walk himself into exhaustion. If he was going to stay alive, he had to get some rest. A taxi clattered by but he ignored it. The tubes were still running. Count the pennies Callan. He was going to need them. The only place he could go to was that all-night Turkish bath up west, and those places cost money. Full of queers too. Maybe he could pick up a rich boy friend. It wouldn't be any worse, he thought, than letting Lonely steal for him.

5

Lonely hated getting up early after a job. A good lie-in, that was the thing, then round to the caff for a bacon sandwich before the pubs opened. But this time he had to stir himself; he'd promised Mr. Callan. Lucky that stupid git in Highgate had a full wallet, he'd only have to draw fifty out of the Post Office.

He yawned and reached for his clothes, then remembered, and stumbled over to the sink instead. The geezer most likely to have a gun for him was Harry Head, known to his intimates as Nutter. Lonely was not one of his intimates, but he did know that Harry had strict ideas about personal hygiene. He gave himself an all-over wash, and used plenty of aftershave. Harry Head was fussy.

Nice place he had though, thought Lonely. Very nice place. One of those fancy boxes you talked into at the door, when the feller asked your name and you give it and he pressed the buzzer and you were let in. Smooth lift, and corridor with carpets, and the door opened by Dougie who was Harry's minder, big feller, like minders always are. Used to be a wrestler; called himself Professor Pain. Doing quite well as a villain he was, but Harry paid him more money. Lonely wiped his feet very carefully and went inside. Dougie didn't speak a word; not even good morning, but that didn't worry Lonely, not at first. Minders never did have much to say for themselves.

Harry was in the room he called his study; books with leather bindings, fancy writing table, mahogany chair. It would take me four nights' thieving just to pay for his suit, thought Lonely, and stood, appropriately humble, waiting for Nutter to finish writing.

'Don't sit down,' Nutter said.

'No, Mr. Head,' said Lonely, and was suddenly aware that Dougie was standing behind him. Nutter put down his pen at last.

'Well?' he said.

'I've come to ask a favour, Mr. Head,' said Lonely.

'You've come to ask for a gun,' said Nutter.

Lonely was so astonished he forgot to be polite.

'How did you find out?' he asked.

'I used my crystal ball,' said Nutter. 'The answer's no.'

He picked up his pen; the interview was over.

'I'm paying top whack, Mr. Head,' said Lonely.

'No,' said Nutter. 'You're not. Because I'm not selling. Not to you. That mate of yours, that Callan – he's poison. And you're not much better, so go away and don't bother me. Right? Don't call us, we'll call you.'

'But Mr. Head–'

'Take him out Dougie,' said Nutter.

A hand like a ham fastened on Lonely's collar, then lifted till his feet were dangling.

'You don't have to,' Lonely said. 'I'm going.'

'That's right,' Nutter said. 'And you're not coming back. Not till you've changed your friends.' He went back to his writing. 'Put him out,' he said again.

Lonely left in a manner that was both painful and undignified. The lack of dignity he could live with, but the pain was intense. Dougie saw to that.

He found a cafeteria and bought himself a cup of tea, four sugars. After a shock like he'd had, he needed them. As he carried the tea to a table, he saw how much his hand was trembling. Dougie really did know how to hurt. And that git Nutter. Where did he get off? Put him out, Dougie... Don't call us we'll call you. Bleeding big-shots. They were all alike. But wait a minute. Somebody had warned Nutter off. Told him about Mr. Callan. And Nutter had done what this somebody had said. Even when he'd offered to pay top whack. So that somebody must be even bigger than Nutter and that somebody very definitely had it in for Mr. Callan – and by the look of it for anybody daft enough to try to help Mr. Callan. It was time he told Mr. Callan goodbye. Look at last night, Lonely thought. Broke into me gaff, ate half me supper, then asked for money. Bloody near all I got. And even when I said he could have it he put his hands on me. And insulted me. He's no better than Dougie...

Then he thought, No, that's wrong. He's a bloody sight worse. One of the blokes Callan had fought in the nick had been Dougie's size, and Dougie's nature, and Mr. Callan had hurt him bad. Put him in the hospital – just using his hands. Stuff they taught you in the Commandos. Japanese-sounding stuff. Not that Mr. Callan had ever used it on him. You got to be fair. Used it on Rinty though. That Glasgow git who was going to carve me. Slipped me a few quid when I was broke, too. Good mate, Mr. Callan. Share his last penny. Take a chance for you an' all. That Rinty carried a razor... Oh, Christ, Lonely thought. I'm going to have to try again. If only Mr. Callan hadn't been so nice to him. That was what made it so bloody unfair.

The best bet, he thought, was Manny Mendel. Manny ran a fish and chip shop so he could pay his taxes, but he was a fence as well, and he could get you things. He charged high, but he was reliable. You could say that for him. Trouble was he lived out

Bermondsey way. Even the bus fares were costing a fortune...

The shop was shut when he got there, so he waited. Lonely was used to waiting for the attention of more important people. It was a part of life. He bought a paper and looked at the horses, and picked one out for Haydock Park that was a certainty at eleven to two, only he couldn't bet on it because he had to get a magnum revolver .38 calibre and the ammo to go with it. There was no bleeding justice, he thought, not for the first time, but the thought didn't really upset him. Injustice was a part of life too, like having to wait for Manny... When he turned up at last he was driving a big, beaten up old Ford. A bloke who could have had a Rolls Royce. Which just goes to show how wide he was, thought Lonely. In Manny's line of business it didn't pay to draw attention to yourself.

He watched as Manny reached inside the back of the car and hefted out a sack of potatoes. Manny was a fat man, but there was muscle on him. The potatoes didn't bother him at all. Lonely walked up to the shop door as Manny fumbled for his key.

'Could I have a word, Mr. Mendel?' Lonely said.

Mendel didn't even look round. 'No,' he said.

Stuck up bastard, thought Lonely. He stinks of grease.

'It's a matter of business,' he said.

Methodical, unhurried, Mendel put down the potato-sack, went through his pockets until he found the shop door key and put it in the lock. Then he turned to Lonely.

'No business,' he said. 'Not with you – and especially not with that crazy mate of yours.'

'I'm paying good money,' said Lonely.

'Maybe,' said Mendel. 'But not to me.'

'You been warned off?' said Lonely.

'Put it this way,' said Mendel. 'A lot of my people were prophets in the old days. Some of them in a good way of business. I'm in a good way of business too – and today I'm a prophet. Specially for you. The Book of Manny Mendel, chapter one, verse one. You listening, Lonely?'

'Yes, Mr. Mendel.'

'You come bothering me again and you'll have a very nasty accident. End of prophecy.'

Mendel picked up his sack of potatoes; the door slammed in Lonely's face.

Surely that was the end of it? The word was out. No guns for Mr. Callan. If Nutter wouldn't help and Manny wouldn't help, then that was it. They were the biggest suppliers there were, so if they were scared the rest would be terrified. He might just as well stick a few bob on that nag at Haydock Park. He'd tried hard enough. Mr. Callan couldn't say he hadn't tried. But there was nothing

63

else he could do... He caught a bus and went back to the racing form. Orphan Annie – five to four... Waste of money... Sunset, nine to two... You must be joking... The Count, a hundred to eight... The Count. It was a horse he'd never heard of, but the name bothered him. Suddenly Lonely remembered the Polisher, and the woman sitting next to him sniffed, sniffed again, then moved to another seat. Lonely didn't even know she'd gone; just sat there hating himself for remembering the Polisher's existence and the fact that he might – just might – give Lonely what he wanted, because the Polisher was like Mr. Callan. You could warn him all you wanted but he'd do exactly what he wanted to do – and chance the consequences.

The Polisher's name was Adam. Adam Komorowski, or some such bloody gibberish, and the word was that he actually had been a count back in Poland before the war. Came over here with the Polish Air Force. Got medals for that. And after the war was over he stayed on. In Soho. As bent as a fish-hook, and he'd made a fortune at it, because he wasn't afraid of anything, that one. What he wanted he took, and if you tried to stop him he'd kill you. Semi-retired now, they said. But guns were the Polisher's speciality; always had been. If he wanted to get one, he'd get it.

Lonely got off the bus at Piccadilly and

found a phone booth. His Aunty Glad would know where the Polisher was. His Aunty Glad knew everything – and besides, she'd worked in a strip club the Polisher used to own – before she went on the batter... Lonely dialled, heard her answer, then took a deep breath and shoved the coin in.

'Count Komorowski?' Aunty Glad said.

'That's right.'

'You must be barmy. What d'you want to go bothering him for?'

'Cos I got to,' said Lonely.

It took a lot of arguing – lot of lying come to that – but in the end she told him.

Callan left the Turkish Baths and set about killing time till Lonely got the gun. The day was warmer, warm enough to sit in the park – read something. There was a new book on Wellington he could get – except books cost money and he didn't know what looking at print might do to his eyes. Walking would only make him more hungry, and he was starving already. The Turkish Bath had been a good idea – if it hadn't cost so much. A lot of steam, needle-shower, then a working over by a masseur with hands like bulldozers' grabs – and after that sleep, right through the night, secure and undisturbed. But at the end of it all he woke up hungry, so that in the end he had to go to a self-service place – had to – and eat his way through soup, steak and

65

kidney pie and mash and roly-poly pudding. Pretty terrible really, but at least it was filling. Then he walked for a bit and went to the cinema, and saw the same show three times, changing his seat so that the usherette wouldn't spot him and ask him to leave. Cowboys fighting wicked Mexicans. Amateur stuff. If he'd been a wicked Mexican there wouldn't have been a cowboy alive after twenty minutes.

When it was time he left the cinema and made his way to the market where Lonely's Aunty Gertie had her coffee-stall. Surely to God, he thought, I'll be safe going there? They may be watching Lonely's place, but they can't watch all his relatives. It would take an army. And I never knew anybody who could tail Lonely when he didn't want to be tailed. But then, he thought, I don't know the men who are coming to kill me. Maybe they're that good. So he went to the market with a caution that was almost obsessive, but he went. The gun made that inevitable.

It was a cheerful, noisy place: the men behind the stalls chatting up the women customers with a sort of cheerful lewdness, and the women, or some of them, the ones who liked an audience, giving back as good as they got. Noise, and rotted vegetables under foot, and everywhere great splashes of colour from oranges, apples, grapes, glowing against mounds of potatoes or great piles of beans. Then the butchers, raw meat behind glass, and white coats smeared with red, the bloke who sold canned goods with no labels on them– Only five pence missus and pick where you like. Every time a prize – then flowers and second-hand books, a black man selling gadgets that would do everything except work, and Indians with mounds of rice for sale, and curry powder that brought the hunger back every time you smelled it, till at last he got to Aunty Gertie's coffee-bar. More of a shack really. Built of solid wooden planking with a let-down counter and Aunty presiding over it, flanked by menacing urns of coffee and tea that steamed and belched like volcanoes getting ready for the big per-formance. Callan walked round to the back of the shed, and at once the door opened. He went in to a space about the size of a broom cupboard, and found he was sharing it with Lonely, a sink and drainer, and about four hundred cups, which Lonely was washing and drying with frantic speed. Aunty's busi-ness was brisk and her temper uncertain. Callan picked up a dishtowel and set to work.

'Get it?' he asked.

Lonely shook his head. Around them the noise of the market racketed and throbbed; shouts, sales-talk, and laughter, the rattle of a lorry's clapped-out engine, unhappy in re-verse.

Callan said softly, 'It didn't have to be a magnum. I told you. Any gun that worked.'

Lonely said, 'Mr Callan – I couldn't get you a water-pistol.'

'Come on,' said Callan. 'There's plenty of guns about if you pay for them.'

'Not for you, Mr. Callan,' Lonely said. 'I offered top whack. Honest. They turned me down.'

'How many did you try?' Callan asked.

'Two,' said Lonely. The best two in the trade–'

'Two?' Callan said. 'You're not going to die of overwork are you? Blimey, there must be dozens.'

'Mr Callan believe me,' Lonely said. 'These two are the biggest. They're important. Even for them to see me is like doing me a favour – and they don't want to see me.'

'One of the others might be a bit less fussy,' said Callan.

'No,' said Lonely. 'They won't. And I'll tell you why, Mr. Callan. They knew I was after a gun before I even asked – and they knew I was after it for you.'

'They knew my name?' said Callan.

'Better than they know their own,' said Lonely. 'They've been warned off, Mr. Callan, and they're scared. And anyone who can scare them – I don't want nothing to do with them, Mr. Callan. I tell you straight.'

Aunty Gertie yelled for more cups then,

and Callan was silent until Lonely opened the serving hatch and passed them through, then shut the hatch.

'You think everybody's been warned off?' he asked.

'I know they have,' said Lonely. 'Look – I saw a geezer who fences for me on my way here. He gets the odd piece from time to time and I tried to have a word with him. You know what happened?'

'You better tell me,' said Callan.

'He was off across the road without even looking to see what was coming. Nearly walked under a bus. Mr. Callan – I scared him worse than the traffic.' For a moment Lonely surrendered to the thought that he had scared somebody. 'Honest, Mr. Callan,' he said at last, 'the best thing you can do is run. You're bad news.'

Callan thought, Run? Just give me the chance. You tried, old son, and you failed. No. That's not fair either. You tried and Hunter knew you'd try, and fixed it so that you couldn't possibly succeed.

Lonely said, 'I did try one other geezer.'

'He turned you down, too?'

'I don't know,' said Lonely. 'We had a bit of a talk. In the Rutland Club.'

'The where?' said Callan.

No wonder he's surprised, thought Lonely. Me in the Rutland Club, the poshest place in Saint James's. But he'd rung up the number

69

his Aunty Glad had given him, and this cut-glass voice had said Rutland Club, and he'd asked for Count Komorowski like his Aunty had told him. And the Polisher had told him to come on over. They'd sat in a room full of books – he'd seen more books that day than in all the rest of his life put together – and a geezer in a striped waistcoat had brought them sherry, which had turned out to be as bad as Lonely had always suspected it would be. Like swallowing tin-tacks. Anyway the Polisher had listened.

'He wants to see you,' Lonely said.

'Does he?' said Callan. 'Who is he?'

'I always used to call him the Polisher,' said Lonely. 'His name's Komorowski. Some sort of a Lord he used to be. He said he knows you.'

'Yeah,' said Callan. 'We've met.'

'Business?' Lonely asked.

'Yeah. Business. Did he say he would get me a gun?'

'All he said was he wanted a chat. Mind you he didn't say he wouldn't get you one.'

'Where am I supposed to meet him?' Callan asked.

'He'll pick you up by the pub on the corner. Seven o'clock. He said – wait a minute now – he said, "Tell your friend he has nothing to fear from this invitation. He has my word on that." You going to see him, Mr. Callan?'

'Yeah. I'll see him.'

'Suppose he's lying?'

'He's never broken his word in his life,' Callan said. 'Mind you, it's about the only thing he hasn't broken.'

'He looked a hard one,' said Lonely.

'Like you wouldn't believe,' said Callan.

6

Komorowski drove up in a Rolls Royce. It was middle-aged, good-looking, and beautifully preserved. Like its owner, thought Callan. Five years since I've seen him, and he hasn't aged five days. Hair thick and prematurely white, lean, hard body, handsome Slav face full of that brooding romantic melancholy that could still make seven women out of ten come running. Also a gangster, a murderer and a thief, although that wasn't my business – not until he thought he'd try his hand at political assassination. Then it was very much my business – and Hunter's.

'You don't look very well,' Komorowski said.

'You do,' said Callan.

'That is because I take good care of myself.'

Callan looked over his shoulder, seeking for following cars. 'Where are we going?' he asked.

'I thought we might perhaps have a bite together.'

'Suits me,' said Callan. The steak and kidney pie had occurred far too long ago.

'Your club?'

Komorowski laughed.

'No,' he said. 'Not the club. I do not think you would be appropriate there.'

You're damn right, thought Callan. Hunter's a member.

'You found Lonely appropriate?' he asked aloud.

'I found him amusing,' said Komorowski, 'in such surroundings. Life is so often dull these days that I find amusement a very rare thing.'

'Are you getting any now?' Callan asked.

'I'm trying to,' said Komorowski.

They drove to a place in Knightsbridge, a place Komorowski owned. He drove the car to the mews behind it, into a garage the door of which opened when he pressed a switch on the dashboard. Another door led to a flight of stairs, and the warm, deep-carpeted ambience of a place where the rich came to eat. Komorowski led the way to an office, and went inside. More luxury. The worn and well-used kind that Komorowski had once taken for granted – and was taking for granted again.

'We won't be disturbed here,' Komorowski said, then went to a window and looked down into the street. 'I don't think we were followed.'

'Not this time,' said Callan, and Komorowski caught the tremor in his voice.

'So now you know about fear,' he said. 'Somehow I never expected you to know fear so well.'

'It happens,' Callan said.

Komorowski pressed a button, a waiter appeared, and they ordered food. While the waiter was out of the room, they talked; while he was in it, they sat in silence. Neither Komorowski nor the waiter seemed to find this at all unusual.

'You taught me about fear,' Komorowski said.

'Come off it,' said Callan. 'You'd been chancing your arm since the war.'

'It was not at all the same thing,' Komorowski said. 'When the war began, my father was killed almost at once. Killed in a charge at the head of a cavalry regiment some idiot on the staff had thought might be a match for a squadron of tanks. My mother soon after was involved with the Resistance – and suffered for it considerably. I was in England, and it was very soon evident that I might never see my mother again. I was an only child. I had loved my parents very much. Being a qualified pilot, I was able to join the Air Force and kill Germans, which is what I wanted to do. I was good at it.

'When the war ended the Russians took over my country – and everything I possessed. Wealth is important to me. Life, I thought, was not. So it was necessary to get money quickly. I became a criminal. A violent one. And I made money because people were afraid of me. They were violent people mostly, but I was more violent. Also I took risks, big risks. They thought I didn't care whether I lived or died. And so did I. I had thought the same thing when I flew Spitfires. I deceived myself. In everything I did I had to have some chance, some edge, however small. And always I used that chance.

'Then I met you – do you remember? It was the day before I was going to kill Von Sturmer, the man who had tortured my mother. He became a civil servant after the war and had come to London on a visit. And I was going to kill him. No fancy confrontations; no drum-head court martial in front of an ageing group of old Resistance Poles who hadn't even seen their own country for thirty years. Just walk in on him when he was alone, shoot him dead and walk away. And go back to my life of crime.

'Only you came to see me. We talked in that club I used to run. I'd just had a new suit delivered from my tailor in Savile Row. My first thought was that you were the worst-dressed killer I'd ever seen. My next was that you were by far the most dangerous. In five minutes you convinced me that if I killed Von Sturmer you would kill me. There was no question of it in my mind. If you came after me I would have no chance, no edge; none at all. And I knew it. With the result that Von Sturmer lived and went back to Germany, and for all I know is still alive and well.'

'He's doing all right,' said Callan. 'Last year they promoted him.'

'He owes it all to you,' said Komorowski, 'because you taught me about fear. And now somebody has taught you.'

'Like you said – you've got to have some edge.'

'And now you have none at all?' Komorowski put down his fork, poured wine. 'Do I understand that your – department has rejected you?'

'Section,' said Callan. 'They call it a section... Yeah. They've rejected me.'

'And intend to kill you?'

'To let me be killed.'

'By the Russians?'

Callan sipped at his wine.

'You know a hell of a lot about it,' he said.

'I worked it out,' Komorowski said. 'It was very easy. A young man called Meres came to see me.

'He said that under no circumstances was I to supply you with a gun, and I went through all the tedious antics expected of me – outraged innocence, law-abiding businessman, loyal – if naturalised – subject of the queen. He found it amusing, but I didn't. He knew a great deal about my activities. Things that Scotland Yard doesn't even suspect. If I give you a gun – Scotland Yard will get the lot.'

'Did he say he'd warned off other suppliers as well?'

'He did,' said Komorowski. '"No guns for Callan." Those were his exact words. He said them with what I can only describe as relish... Then a few days later, Lonely rang me at the club, and I told him to see me there. It really was amusing.'

'Didn't he smell?' Callan asked.

'I took good care not to frighten him. I wanted to see you.'

'To give me a gun?'

Komorowski said, 'I told you that I had deduced that the Russians were mixed up in this. Now let me tell you how. My mother is still alive in Poland. A few days ago I had a letter from her, the first for twenty years. If I help you, reprisals will be taken against her. I am quite sure of it.'

'So no gun,' said Callan.

'I loved her very much,' Komorowski said. 'Now she is hardly even a memory. A certain perfume that one can still buy, the sound of a silk dress as it brushes the floor. Do you know I cannot even be sure whether her eyes are blue or grey? Next year she will be eighty.' Komorowski wiped his lips with his napkin, then rang for the waiter.

'I'm sorry,' he said. 'No gun.'

Coffee came, and brandy of a kind that Callan had never even known existed.

'You certainly know how to soften bad

news,' he said.

'Please don't think I invited you here out of malice,' Komorowski said. 'I said that you taught me about fear – and it is true. But the knowledge was extremely valuable to me. I cannot give you a gun, but I can tell you how to get one.'

'Not in this country you can't.'

'I didn't say it would be in this country. Do you object to going abroad?'

'I don't. The Section will.'

'I'm willing to risk that. But there are conditions.'

'Let's hear them.'

'I'll get you out to a place where I have interests – substantial interests. It's a very nice place. A villa in the sun. Warm beach – private of course – blue sea. I sound like a travel brochure – but it really does have these things. And many of the women are beautiful. You could be happy there–'

'I believe you,' Callan said.

'–But you would be working for me. I'm getting old, Callan. My bones need warming. Also my luck can't last for ever. It's time I moved to a country where all the police take bribes. I've been selling out here for some time. But there are still a few loose ends to tie up. Your job would be to go ahead as a kind of advance-party.'

'What about your mother?'

'No-one knows we've seen each other. If

78

you disappear, how can I be blamed?'

'Lonely knows.'

'He can be dealt with.'

'No,' said Callan.

'I wasn't suggesting that we kill him. You could take him with you. No doubt he can make himself useful.'

'Tell me about the job,' said Callan.

'Bodyguard mostly,' Komorowski said. 'For that I will pay you twenty thousand a year – in cash. From time to time it might be necessary for you to kill someone. For that I would pay a bonus, naturally.'

'What sort of business are you in then?' Callan asked.

'The stupidity business,' Komorowski said. 'Vice, prostitution, drugs. You wouldn't be involved in that side of it.'

'Wouldn't I?'

'Is it possible that you would refuse this offer?'

'Yeah,' said Callan. 'It's possible.'

'You would sooner die?'

'I'd sooner take my chance,' said Callan.

Komorowski said, 'But you told me yourself – you have no chance at all.' He smiled, and there was affection in his smile, and bewilderment too. 'Even now you function according to some sort of code, some system of morality. Don't you realise that you're the only one? Think of Meres, Callan. Think of the Russians and their threats against my mother. Think of the head of your Section. What honour do they have? What honour have I? I'm giving you a chance to live.'

Callan finished his brandy.

'I'm sorry,' he said. 'I can't take it.'

'You're a fool,' Komorowski said, 'and you're going to die. I rather wish you weren't. Goodbye Callan.'

'Goodbye,' Callan said. 'Mind how you go.'

From him that advice was bitter. But at least Komorowski had given him an idea, and if it worked, he'd have a gun.

It was a little box of a house, but it was Chelsea, and the most fashionable part at that. Toby, like Hunter, had private means, and he enjoyed them. Eighteenth-century mews cottage painted white as sugar-icing, door red as blood, a tub of flowers on either side. Callan didn't fancy the door; the lock was too good, and if he knocked Toby would put the chain on before he opened up; he had to. It was part of the drill. Lights on in the drawing-room, so it was round the back for Callan, and take his chance at the tradesmen's entrance... Good lock there, too, but one you could work on, if you had time, and a set of keys you'd made yourself.

Patiently Callan explored the lock, sensitive as a lover, coaxing and gentle. Never try rape on a lock, the bloke at Bartram's had told him. It'll seize up worse than a woman.

You've got to soothe them, son. And Callan soothed this one, wary for coppers and the nosiness of neighbours, while a beat-group throbbed from a nearby discotheque, till it yielded at last with a tiny click he had to strain to hear, but after that it was his, the key turned, the door swung softly open, and he was in.

Kitchen. Glittering as an operating theatre. No mess, no rubbish, Toby didn't eat in all that much... Callan moved silently to the door that led to the living-room. Once he went through that, everything had to be right. He stood by it concentrating, alert for the slightest sound, and a chair creaked at last, there was the sound of liquid pouring, the swish of a soda syphon. About as good as he could hope for. If Toby had the glass to his mouth it would slow him up that much more. Callan breathed slowly and evenly, forcing his body to calmness. Only mugs went in like raving loonies. He looked down at his hands, and waited till they were steady, then grasped the door handle. Now or never, Callan. Move it.

It flung open and he was through it and moving to where Meres sat in his chair before Meres could lower his glass. He sat there in the curve of an open staircase and the bewilderment in his face would have been comical – if there'd been any time for laughter. As it was he hurled the glass away, trying to escape out of an enormous chair like a gigantic egg, as Callan's hand smashed down in a blow that would have ended the thing before it started. It was the girl who saved Meres. She appeared on the staircase as Callan's hand started to move. She wore a dressing gown of Meres', and apparently nothing else, and Callan hadn't even known she existed. His chop mistimed and slammed into the chair, and Meres wriggled free, and threw a fist-strike. But Callan was already swerving from it, spinning round to grab the fist, lever and throw. Meres went through the air in an arc and kept on rolling, sliding from the kick he knew was bound to follow as Callan moved in again, hands ready to grab, and this time Meres grabbed too, they hung on to each other like a couple of judokas at the beginning of a bout, feet dancing for a trip that could be turned into a throw.

Out of the corner of his eye Meres saw the girl reach for the telephone at the head of the stairs.

'No don't,' he yelled. 'Leave it. Stay quiet.' And again Callan threw him, again he rolled away, only this time his shoulder hit the chair like a gigantic egg and his swerve was too slow. Callan's hand moved in a three finger strike to the spot just below the breast bone, and Meres became a rubber man, no movement left in his body. The one that put him out, the chop behind the ear with the edge of the hand, he didn't even feel. Callan looked up, chest heaving, to where the girl still stood by the phone.

'Get away from there,' he said. 'You heard Toby.'

'You – you–' the girl said. Her body was shaking, and the dressing-gown wasn't doing much to cover it, but she was too scared to notice. Any moment now she was going to scream.

'Cover yourself up,' said Callan. 'You look disgusting.'

It was like a slap in the face. The girl's head jerked back, then her hands were busy as she looked down at him.

'That's better,' said Callan. 'Now come down here.' She made no move. 'Am I going to have to come up and get you?'

She started down the stairs then, and circled warily away from Callan.

'You've killed him,' she said.

'Not a chance,' Callan said. 'Just given him a headache, that's all. What's your name?'

'Susan Marsden,' she said.

'You better sit down Susan Marsden,' Callan said. 'You've had a bit of a shock.'

She backed away to a chair and sat primly, knees together, watching as Callan went through Toby's pockets. No gun. Not on him. You wouldn't expect that when he had a bird in, but he must have one somewhere. He'd have to look for it. He said to the girl,

'Known Toby long?'

'A few weeks,' she said, and became aware of her dressing-gown. It was slipping again.

Callan began to work on the cupboards and drawers in the living room. Nothing. Not even a catapult.

'He looks awfully bad,' the girl said.

Callan looked across at Meres: white-faced, the bruise already dark on his neck.

'You should see him when he's conscious,' he said.

'You don't like him very much, do you?' the girl asked.

'How did you guess?'

'Neither do I,' she said, 'but he's a super lover.'

Callan looked at her more sharply. She wasn't having much success adjusting the dressing gown.

'What you on, love?' he asked.

'That's a perfectly foul thing to say.'

'A lot of people think I'm a perfectly foul feller.'

'You beat up Toby.' Her voice showed surprise rather than accusation. 'He's awfully strong.'

Callan went on searching.

Suddenly the girl said, 'I had a smoke. That's not being on anything. Everybody smokes.'

'Toby doesn't,' said Callan. 'He get it for you?'

Her head nodded. She was suddenly ready for sleep. Pot worked like that on some people.

'No speed?' Callan asked. 'No jab in the arm?'

'Not tonight,' she said. 'Tonight I had a smoke.'

'Good, was it?'

'Acapulco Gold,' she said. 'The purest one there is. It works so much better–' Her head fell forward. She was asleep.

Callan used a couple of ties on Meres. When he'd finished Toby couldn't move. Good silk is tough stuff, and Cardin and Saint Laurent use only the best, so Toby would await his pleasure. He looked at the girl. She was out like a light. Time to look for a gun. He set about it methodically, room by room. Little boxes like those didn't have many hiding-places but there had to be one somewhere. Kitchen, drawing-room, dining-room, bedrooms, bathroom. He went through them all... Not a damned thing. But Meres had the same problems as he'd had, and keeping a gun handy was one of them. He stood on the upstairs landing. There was a trap-door leading to the eaves. He pulled a chair across and scrambled up and through, and found it almost at once, under the water-tank; a heavy metal box, just like his own. Locked, just as his had been. He used his keys on it and found that, like his, it was empty.

To give way to rage would be a futile waste of strength. Callan went back to the living-room, past the sleeping girl, and picked up the soda-syphon. Might as well talk to Toby, he thought, and pressed. The syphon was nearly empty by the time Toby stirred, spluttered, and tried to move. Then he saw Callan, and the rage was there at once.

'You bastard,' he said.

'Where is it Toby?' Callan asked.

'I don't know what you're talking about.'

'I'm talking about a gun,' said Callan. 'Your gun. I want it.'

'You haven't a hope in hell,' said Meres. 'Surely you've got the message by now? No guns for Callan.'

'Yours will do.'

'No chance.'

'I can make you,' said Callan.

'Thumbscrews?'

'Didn't bring them,' Callan said. 'A phone call will do. To Hunter.'

'About what?'

'About her,' said Callan, and jerked his thumb at the girl. 'About Susan Marsden, who smokes Acapulco Gold because it's pure. And nice, kind Toby Meres who gets it for her. It'll look great on your Section Report, Toby old boy. Hunter will love it– Or are you trying to tell me he knows?'

'He doesn't,' said Meres. 'If he did he'd

crucify me. But I can't give you my gun.'

'Suit yourself,' said Callan. 'Excuse me. I've got a call to make.'

He rose, and Meres said, 'Wait.' The word was wrenched out of him. Callan waited.

'I can't give you my gun because I haven't got one,' said Meres.

'Come off it Toby,' Callan said, and went to the phone.

'It's true I tell you. This thing's set up so that you can't win.'

'Go on,' said Callan.

'You've tried to get a gun already, haven't you? You wouldn't have come here otherwise.'

'That's right.'

'And you failed, didn't you? Because I put the word out. No guns for you – or that stinking little friend of yours. Hunter planned it all himself so that nothing can go wrong. And nothing will. He has to bring this off, Callan–'

'Where's your gun, Toby?'

'At the Section,' Meres said. 'And it stays there till this is over. Hunter remembered that you know where I live. He thought there might be a chance you'd come here.'

'And he thought I might beat you? And you didn't believe him?'

'All right. You beat me,' said Meres. 'You'll still die.'

'They're here now, aren't they?' Callan

said. 'Those Russians?'

'They're here,' said Meres. 'Hunter briefed them this evening.'

'I'd better be off then,' Callan said, went to the door then came back. 'I almost forgot,' he said, and took out Meres' wallet. A few quid and a load of credit cards. This is the way the rich lived these days. He put the money in his pocket.

'So you've gone back to stealing,' said Meres.

'Stealing?' said Callan. 'What nonsense. This is strictly a loan. If I don't pay it back you can sue my executors.'

He put the money in his pocket, then went upstairs again, found a suitcase, filled it with underwear, shirts, shaving-gear, ties, and came back to Toby.

'Hunter will have this collected for you,' he said.

'You can bet on it,' said Meres.

'You know, Toby,' Callan said, 'it's almost impossible to describe how much you nauseate me,' and looked at the sleeping girl. 'But then I expect people tell you that all the time.'

He left then, not hurrying, but not idling either. The fight with Meres had gone on far too long. Already he had the beginnings of a headache, but all the same he had to look for a room, before the double-vision came back.

7

The night-porter found him some pills for the headache, but for the double-vision he had to go the hospital. There was no other way, and he knew it. He had to leave Meres' case and take a cab. With his eyes in the state they were a street was as lethal as a pistol, so he rode there and watched twin-drivers weave their way past buses, lorries, cars, all in identical pairs, and he sat and worried, and wondered why he hadn't killed Meres, while he had the chance. After all, it was what he had threatened to do. Maybe it was because the girl was there, sleeping off her smoke. When she woke up she'd have found nice, kind Toby dead. Komorowski would have loved that one...

The cab turned in at the gates and Callan paid him off, his hands fumbling with money that never seemed to be precisely where his eyes told him it was ... Komorowski wouldn't have loved that so much. Twenty thousand a year for a bodyguard who could never hope to hit what he aimed at... They even had to find a nurse to guide him to his doctor's surgery. Pretty little thing. A student. She treats me like an old man, thought Callan. Maybe it's because I look like one. She handed him over to Nurse Somerset, and left him. Two Nurse Somersets.

'What's wrong, Mr. Callan?' she asked. 'Double vision again?'

Callan nodded. The two lovely faces looked at him sternly. 'You haven't been exerting yourself, have you?'

'The doctor told me I shouldn't,' Callan said.

'You're quite sure?'

Callan thought of Meres, flat on the floor, a bruise like a birthmark on his neck.

'Do I look like a mug?' he said.

'There's no need to be rude, Mr. Callan,' she said.

Callan said, 'I'm sorry. It's just this thing bothers me you see, nurse.'

'I'll give you the drops,' she said.

She went to a table with a neat row of ampoules and glass jars on it, getting the stuff ready, and as she did so the doctor came out, pulling on his coat, then checked when he saw Callan.

'You're back quick,' he said, and peered into Callan's eyes. 'Over-exertion?'

Nurse Somerset said, 'I asked him doctor. He says not.' She put down one ampoule, picked up another.

'I hope you mean it,' said the doctor.

The icy coldness in his eyes was bliss.

'Don't forget our date next month,' the

doctor said. Callan heard him go, and his eyes saw nothing but the swimming wetness the drops created, bright and pure as Northern Seas. He lay back, sighing his relief.

'That's all very well,' Nurse Somerset said, 'but those drops won't work for ever.'

'The doctor said a month,' said Callan.

'If you're lucky. After that you really will have to lie up.'

'I'd be glad to,' said Callan, and meant it.

When the moisture cleared she was looking at him with an expression he thought he could never read, or maybe it was just beauty. She was unbelievably beautiful, face and body perfect, no movement, no glance without its own peculiar grace. She looked elegant, he thought, but with an elegance more subtle, more ancient, than that of Paris, or even Rome. Ancient Egypt, he thought. The young queen he'd seen pictures of. Eyes just as dark, wide-staring; the same high-bridged, arrogant, perfect nose; skin with just that golden glow.

'Where do you come from?' he asked.

'Barbados.'

'Do they all look like you there?'

'No,' she said. 'A lot of them look like you.'

'Maybe that sounded as if I was being rude again,' said Callan. 'I didn't mean to be.'

She gave him that same enigmatic look.

'I believe you, Mr. Callan,' she said. 'I didn't mean to be rude either,' then picked up his form, marked it up and walked to a filing cabinet.

'Are you still at the same address?' she asked.

'Not all the time,' said Callan. 'Why?'

'There may be a cancellation on the doctor's list of operations,' she said. 'If there is we might have to let you know quickly to get you in here.'

'I'm moving around a bit,' said Callan. 'Staying with different friends. You don't enjoy being on your own at a time like this.'

Nurse Somerset said sharply, 'Mr Callan, we're talking about an operation to save your sight. We must know where we can reach you.'

Callan gave her Lonely's number. If there were a cancellation, and he lasted that long, he'd be as safe in a hospital as anywhere else; and when his eyes were bandaged he'd be in a ward full of people.

'Thank you,' Nurse Somerset said. 'How's the vision now?'

'Fine,' said Callan. 'Thanks very much. Can I go now?'

'If you're sure it's clear. You can sit a while if you want to.'

She took off her overall. Beneath it she wore a dress of a pink like peonies, that made her skin more beautiful than ever, then took her coat from a peg behind the door. Callan held it for her.

'I told you to sit still,' she said.

Callan said, 'I wouldn't call this over-exerting myself.'

Her smile warmed his day.

'You finished now?' he asked.

'Lunch,' she said.

'Have it with me,' said Callan. She hesitated.

'Look,' Callan said, 'this thing doesn't affect my appetite.'

Or only when I'm scared, he added to himself.

'I eat in half an hour,' she said. 'I use the rest of the time for reading.'

'So I'll eat in half an hour,' Callan said. 'Where would you like to go?'

'Where I usually go,' she said. 'The pub round the corner. No. Maybe not. That's always full of hospital people. Let's try another one.'

They walked out together down long corridors, then out through gloomy gates. She didn't talk much, and she didn't make the going easy for him either. Looks like that one smile is my ration for the day, Callan thought. When he took her arm as they crossed the street he could feel her muscles tense.

So that's it, he thought. She thinks I'm after a beer and a sandwich – and a quick rape for dessert. But maybe if you look like that you get to expect it.

93

Aloud he said, 'You think I'm going to start over-exerting myself again.'

No smile, this time; but her arm relaxed.

'The Greyhound' was a posh pub for posh people. None of your hoi polloi. This was for managerial types with stiff collars, and trousers that matched their suits. There wasn't much beer being drunk either, Callan noticed. This was your Scotch and water and gin and tonic set, and when somebody put a glass in your hand you said Cheers old man and went on talking. When Miss Somerset walked in she was the only woman in the place, except the barmaid, and they noticed her all right, and nearly broke their necks trying to look without being seen; and they liked what they looked at, thought Callan, only the stupid twits were more embarrassed than pleased. As if it would be perfectly all right, if only it were happening somewhere else.

And the idiots were closing ranks on them too, just as if somebody had given a signal to make it hard for them to get to the bar; punishing Callan for his suit that was more expensive than theirs but needed pressing; punishing her for her coat that was cheap, and her beauty because it wasn't English, and because she made no attempt to hide it. The backs lined up solid, and waited to hear Callan ask, humbly, to be allowed to approach the bar.

Nurse Somerset waited for it too, but somehow it didn't work like that. There were no obvious shovings, and certainly nothing so vulgar as bad language used in anger, but somehow as Callan approached them they moved, and she found herself at the bar and no-one had touched her. Callan ordered the soft drink and sandwiches she asked for, then more sandwiches and beer for himself. The beer arrived in a pewter tankard, which didn't surprise Callan, any more than the fact that it cost a great deal too much. He turned to face her, and the movement gained them more space at the bar.

'Cheers,' he said.

'Thank you,' she said.

Quite an ordinary man on the surface, she thought. The kind you wouldn't want to look at twice, but somehow you did look at him twice – when he wanted you to. And that second look was enough to learn that he was dangerous, or could be. There was a kind of contained power in the man, a feral quality that the neat suits and stiff collars had sensed at once, and envied – and feared. It would be easy to be afraid of this man; it might be equally easy to be in love with him.

'I didn't think it would be like this,' she said.

'Don't you like the sandwiches then?'

This time she laughed aloud.

'That's better,' he said. 'You worry too

much, Nurse Somerset. You don't have to, you know.'

'What makes you think I worry?'

'You wouldn't go to your usual pub because of what people might say–'

'It wasn't you,' she said. 'Honestly it wasn't.'

'I know that,' Callan said. 'It's you. Let me finish. So you drag me to this place and get into a panic because a few twits start looking at you.'

She looked up at him then, furious.

'You don't know what it's like,' she said.

'Maybe I don't,' said Callan. 'You better tell me.'

'My father was a rich man in Barbados,' she said. 'A rich nigger. My mother was almost white, but almost is never quite, Mr. Callan. I was going to be a doctor, but my father died. Broke. All the money he was supposed to have – it looked like it was there; it even felt like it was there. But it was all tied up in deals. And when my father died, the deals died too. We had nothing. And it didn't bother me. Do you believe that?'

'You have so many other things. Of course I believe it,' said Callan. 'Go on.'

'So I became a nurse instead. One day I thought I'd save my money and take my doctor's degree. But it hasn't happened. Not yet. And I'm twenty-eight years old.'

'I like having lunch with older women.

Older than me, I mean.'

She laughed again, but her eyes were angry. 'Please, no jokes,' she said. 'I'm being serious.'

'Be serious then.'

'When you look like me – and you're my colour – men think you're easy. They can be nice about it for a long time, but always tucked away in the back of their minds they have that thought. She's asking for it. She's easy. I'm not easy, Mr. Callan.'

'I'd say you were bloody difficult,' said Callan. 'I'd also say it's part of your charm.' He looked at the clock above the bar. French gilt. It would be.

'Nurse Somerset,' he said, 'or may I call you Nurse?'

'My name's Amanda,' she said. 'I'm not sure I want you to use it.'

'I was just going to tell you your half-hour's up,' Callan said. 'It's time you went back to your reading.'

'It went very quickly,' she said. 'Thank you.'

He finished his beer and led the way out of the bar; the same neat, unhurried performance. Again no man touched her, and the looks didn't seem quite so important this time. She held out her hand.

'I'll see you again,' she said, and he smiled.

'You're going to have to,' he said.

'Perhaps next time I could buy you lunch.'

97

'Perhaps,' he said. 'But there's one thing I'd better mention. Sometimes I can be difficult too.'

It was good to stand and watch her go; the effortless grace, the pride around the fear like a pearl round grit. It was good even to wonder what books she read, but then she turned a corner and was gone, and he was alone again. He still had problems. He rang Lonely at his gaff. There was no answer. In the boozer thought Callan – unless he's helping Aunty again.

He tried the coffee-stall, and Lonely answered.

'It's Callan.'

'Oh hullo,' said Lonely. 'I'm a bit busy like at the moment–'

'Aunty there is she?'

Lonely said, 'That's right. Yeah.'

'I don't suppose you got something for me?'

'I might have,' said Lonely. His voice dropped to a whisper. 'Tell you what – could we meet at me Aunty's?'

'You're at your Aunty's.'

'I mean me Aunty Glad.' He whispered the address so softly that Callan had to strain to hear it.

'You sure it'll be all right?' Callan asked.

'Yeah,' said Lonely. 'No trouble. Six o'clock. I'll see you.'

He put the phone down and found himself

98

looking at his Aunty Gertie through the hatchway.

'I don't pay you to go having chats when you should be working,' she said.

'You haven't paid me at all this week,' said Lonely.

Aunty Gertie glowered, and Lonely began to feel nervous. She had forearms on her like joints of pork.

'I don't want none of your lip,' she said.

'Sorry Aunty.'

'When things quiets down a bit you and me's going to have a talk.'

Things didn't quiet down till after three, but at last they were left unbothered by customers, and Aunty Gertie lifted the counter-flap and lit the gas, put on a kettle and brought out from their hiding place a silver tea-pot, silver tea-spoons, two cups and saucers of Sèvres china. Lonely looked at them unimpressed. She'd been a good whizzer once, and in her time shoplifting wasn't so easy as it was these days, but granted it was nice stuff, she didn't have to go on as if she'd lifted the crown jewels... Aunty warmed the tea-pot, spooned in the Earl Grey. She'd sooner die of thirst than drink the stuff she sold the mugs.

'Did you go down the deli like I asked you?'

Lonely rummaged for and found a neatly wrapped parcel, handed it over and Aunty Gertie opened it.

'Smoked salmon and Ardennes pâté,' she said. 'Just right. You're a good lad Lonely and you'll be a better one after I've got me change.'

Lonely handed it over. But at least the old girl didn't bear grudges.

'Dig in,' she said.

'If it's all the same to you I'd just as soon have a corned beef sandwich,' Lonely said.

'Suit yourself.'

She watched him shake tomato-sauce over the corned beef. 'No class,' she said. 'No class at all.'

Lonely added mustard.

'Who was it phoned you?' Aunty Gertie asked. 'And don't speak with your mouth full.'

Lonely swallowed.

'Mate of mine,' he said.

'Got a lot of mates have you?'

'No,' said Lonely. 'I haven't. You know I haven't.'

'We both know it,' she said. 'What you've got, my lad, is family. Silly perishers like me who have to look out for you, just because I promised your poor mother–'

'I know that Aunty. And I'm grateful. Honest.'

'We'll see about that,' Aunty said. 'Now. Who was it phoned you?'

'I – I'm not at liberty to say,' said Lonely, and waited for the explosion. It didn't come.

Instead his Aunty Gertie was looking at him with something very close to approval.

'That's right, Lonely,' she said. 'Always stand by your mates.' She ate a pâté sandwich, then continued: 'Now I'm going to tell you who called you. That way you won't feel embarrassed. It was that geezer who was round here helping with the washing up.' Lonely said nothing. 'Nice of him that,' said Aunty, 'to come and give a mate a hand. He went off with Count Kornorowski from what I hear.'

'I'm not at liberty to talk about no counts neither.'

'Quite right,' his aunty said again. 'Always keep shtum about him Lonely. I'm warning you.'

'Who told you about him?' Lonely asked.

'Your Aunty Glad,' Aunty Gertie said. 'We had a bit of a chat last night. She tells me the count says you can use her place to meet a feller any time you want. A feller who's a mate of yours. A feller called Callan. And now I hear you arranging to meet a mate of yours at Glad's tonight.'

'So I'm meeting a mate.'

'Callan,' Aunty Gertie said. 'Hard geezer by the look of him. Reminded me of a bloke who did you a favour that time Rinty was after you. Only he had a different name then.'

'A lot of people have different names.'

101

'He should find another one then,' his aunty said, 'because I've been hearing a buzz about this Callan. Needs a gun and can't get one.'

She didn't wait for an answer. Lonely's face was assent enough.

'He's in shtuck, that mate of yours,' Aunty Gertie said. 'It could be dead shtuck – and I don't want you in there with him.'

'I've only got a message for him,' Lonely said.

'I'm going to be honest with you,' said his aunt. 'There's some are born to be heroes, and there's some are born to be cowards.' She hesitated. 'You weren't never born to be a hero, Lonely.'

'But it's only a message,' Lonely said. 'Honest.'

'I got a bad feeling,' his aunty said. 'I think we better see what the leaves has got to say.'

She swirled the tea in Lonely's cup, tipped it carefully over the sink, then looked at the tea-leaves that remained. Lonely sat still, prepared to listen hard. You could say what you liked, when it came to the tea-leaves, Aunty Gertie knew.

'Yes – there's a gun there all right,' she said.

'Do I get it for him?'

She said sharply, 'No you don't. But it's there. And a stick. Trouble with a stick.'

'A cosh like?'

102

'Bigger.' Aunty Gertie said. 'More like a crutch.'

'For me?'

'It doesn't say,' she said. 'But it's your cup.' She looked again. 'Fire too. You got to be careful about a fire.' She put the cup down. 'You never had such a bad cup in your whole life,' she said.

'Isn't there anything good?' he asked.

She could see an anchor. That meant somebody was depending on him, and she knew who that somebody was. It didn't do to lie about the tea-leaves, but you didn't have to tell all the truth either.

'You keep away from that Callan,' she said.

'He's my mate,' said Lonely. 'I got to see him.'

Aunty Gertie thought: That bloody anchor.

Aunty Glad lived near the King's Road, like Meres, but in much grander style, thought Callan. She had the first floor of a house that was a period gem in the style of Adam, *circa* 1780. Just the one floor must have cost her a bomb, Callan thought. They said brasses were sitting on a fortune, but it wasn't everyone that managed to hang on to it. He pressed a button labelled Miss de Courcy Mannering, and a voice of exquisite refinement said 'Yes?' making it into a word of three syllables.

103

'Name of Callan,' said Callan. 'I've come to see Lonely.'

'You may come up,' the voice said.

A nice staircase, old as the house, and polished every day since it was built. Nice door at the top too, smooth as satin, and a nice set of locks on it. Aunty Glad wasn't taking any chances. He rang the bell, and Aunty Glad opened the door at once. She looked like the kind of gentlewoman who came up twice a year to shop at Harrods: all cashmere and pearls and tweeds and low-heeled hand-lasted shoes. Her hair was white and carefully styled, and she was doing a good job of preserving the remains of what must have been a quite remarkable beauty.

She said, 'I hope you remembered to wipe your feet.'

Callan hadn't, but he lied fluently and well. Ex-brass or not, Miss de Courcy Mannering had a formidable hauteur.

'This carpet's an Aubusson,' she said, 'and I won't have it spoiled.'

Callan looked at it, and admired it, and everything else in sight. The lady's drawing-room was furnished with an elegance almost breath-taking. Get rid of the electric light bulbs, he thought, and you could expect Beau Brummell to walk in any minute.

'It's a lovely room,' he said.

'It should be. It cost a fortune. And before we go any further young man, I want to tell

104

you I know everything in this room, so don't think you can half-inch anything of mine.'

'I don't steal,' said Callan.

'Then why does Lonely say he's a mate of yours?'

'Because he is. Look – we met in the nick, and I was doing bird for stealing. But that was a long time ago. I don't steal now.'

'Oh we are proud,' she said.

'Look Miss de Courcy Mannering–'

'Come off it,' she said, her voice losing not one shred of its refinement. 'I'm Lonely's Aunt Glad. That handle was for the customers – the ones that liked a bit of class.'

'Look,' said Callan. 'Lonely asked me to come here because he had some news for me – and that's all I've come for.'

She looked at him, meditative, shrewd: the kind of look, Callan thought, that a butcher might give a steer at Smithfield.

'You're a hard one all right,' she said at last. 'Hard all through. The count was right.'

'I hope he meant it as a compliment,' said Callan.

She ignored it. 'What bothers me is you have Lonely for a mate.'

'That was the nick,' said Callan. 'I wouldn't want him to do a job with me.'

He spoke humbly, as if he were at school again, and the teacher had accused him of leading a smaller boy astray.

'He's easily led, Lonely,' said Aunty Glad.

'Not by me,' said Callan. 'I do my own jobs, thank you very much.'

'What kind of jobs?'

This was too much.

'Mind your own bleeding business,' said Callan.

Then the buzzer sounded, and Callan had to wait in icy silence while the little man was admitted, and asked if he'd wiped his feet.

'Your friend's no gentleman,' Aunty Glad said.

'Well he wouldn't be, would he?' Lonely said.

'I,' said Aunty Glad, 'have been used to mixing with the cream.' She walked to the door. 'You can let yourselves out. The drink's in the commode over there.' She turned back and glowered at Lonely. 'Nick anything and I'll half kill you.'

Then she was gone, and Callan found that he was wiping his forehead.

'Blimey,' he said.

'Caution, isn't she?' said Lonely. 'She likes you though.'

'You're joking.'

'She must do,' said Lonely. 'She said we could have a drink. She never gives me a drink.'

He walked to the commode.

'What'll it be, Mr. Callan?'

'Scotch,' said Callan.

Lonely poured a generous measure, and

handed it to Callan, then found a beer.

'Did you get it?' Callan asked.

'Not exactly,' said Lonely. 'But this geezer said you could have one, so I–'

'What geezer?'

'Name of Judd,' said Lonely. 'Came up to me in the boozer when I was having me lunch-break. I wish there was more money in thieving, Mr. Callan. It's killing, working for Aunty Gertie.'

'Tell me about Judd,' said Callan.

'Thick-set feller,' Lonely said. 'About your height. Scar on his left wrist. Spoke with a sort of accent.'

'What sort of accent?'

'Yankee,' Lonely said. 'He says he knew you wanted a gun. Said he could get you one.'

'He came straight up to you?'

'That's right,' Lonely said. 'Told me he knew we was mates.'

'And who told him?'

'Geezer you'd done a few jobs for. Name of Hunter. Only he said this had nothing to do with Hunter. Said it very particular. Tell him I got a gun, he says. Smith and Wesson Magnum .38 – and all the rounds he needs.'

'Anything else?'

'They done you dirt, he says, but he only found out about it today– But he didn't say who they were. Do you know, Mr. Callan?'

'I know,' said Callan.

'He said to tell you it was a crying bloody shame and he didn't want to get involved but he had to give you a gun on account of you'd always been a good mate. Meet him half past eleven tonight, he says. That building site off the Cromwell Road where they're building that new hotel.'

So that's where I'm supposed to die, thought Callan.

8

The building site looked like the aftermath of a Russian Spring offensive in World War Two. Bulldozers like bogged down tanks lay humped in mud, caissons of concrete, squat and round as pill-boxes, lorries, abandoned equipment; they were all there. Only the vast Meccano spread of steel scaffolding told of construction, rather than destruction, and even that, thought Callan, might be coming down, by the look of it, rather than going up. Cautiously he walked round the enormous, empty site, stark-lit by the high arcs of street lights, cold, menacing. He was frightened, and nothing he could do could dispel the fear, he didn't expect it. But in the past he had learned how fear could be controlled, even used to advantage to put an even finer edge on wariness, to speed reactions already as quick as practice and reflex could make them.

But this time it didn't happen. The fear was so intense he couldn't control it. The only need he could feel was the need to go away from this place, to find warmth, noise, the security of people – except that that would mean the fear would be postponed, not banished, and when it came back it would be more intense than ever. He had to go on. This was his one chance to get a gun, and he had to take it. The man calling himself Judd might, just might, be on his own and if he were Callan might, just might, be able to get his gun from him. If he failed he would die, but then he was going to die anyway, so what difference did it make? Silently, over and over in his mind, he repeated the words: It's not much of a chance, but it's all the chance there is, and at last his mind accepted it: he had to be where he was.

He looked at the building site from across the street. Of all the places he might have found to die in, this seemed the most unlikely. Death belonged in shut-in rooms, inside a car, a hotel corridor, even a prison cell. Only in the early days had it been possible he might die in the open, and then the landscape had been jungle; dim-lit, sticky hot, undergrowth-cluttered, not the stark openness he looked at: Knowles-Martin, Contractors. Site of London's largest hotel. 1,200 Bedrooms. Warning. Guard Dogs on Site. Guard dogs he could cope with. They didn't carry guns... He walked on further past the Clerk of Works' hut, a pile of pipes like a barricade, a heap of trenching spades yellowed with mud. He'd once been on a burial detail that used spades like that...

The voice called softly, 'Callan. Over here,'

and his body reacted as if it had been jerked with wires. The man crouched by a caisson of wet concrete, his body in shadow. A short, thick-set man, like Judd; a man with a mid-Western accent – like Judd. They'd really taken trouble over this one.

He crossed the road and neatly took the low fence that separated the building work from the pavement, then stumbled to hands and knees as he neared the caisson. When he got up again, there was a lump of brick in his hand. The man by the caisson of concrete was still deep in its shadow.

'Judd,' Callan called.

The man made no move.

'Over here,' he said.

Callan moved across towards the caisson, past the comforting shelter of a bulldozer, his footsteps almost silent on mud that was drying hard. As he neared the open space between the bulldozer and the caisson, he called out:

'Did you get a gun?'

'Sure I got it,' the man said. 'Didn't Lonely tell you?'

He was still talking as Callan raced to the open, swerving away from him. He'd got a gun all right: its muzzle was still seeking Callan's heart as he hurled the brick and dropped to his hands and knees like a sprinter waiting for the start. The brick landed not quite where Callan had aimed, but it did damage enough, striking with appalling force at a point just below the man's elbow. He gasped and dropped the gun, but as Callan continued his rush, picked it up left-handed and scrambled up the caisson's ladder. Callan, as he followed, could hear him groan with pain. He reached the top with Callan only a couple of feet behind him. He turned and kicked, but Callan was ready for that, head and shoulder ducked beneath the blow and he slammed a blow at the man's other leg, knocking him off balance as he leaped on to the caisson platform. They circled warily, the other man with one arm dangling useless, Callan all the time aware of his eyes' vulnerability. Of the gun there was no sign.

Got it on him, Callan thought. Under his arm, or his pants' waist-band. You better get on with it boy. Whether he's got mates here or not, this is the best chance you've got.

From a distance he could hear a high, thin whistling sound, but neither he nor the other man allowed it to interfere with their total concentration on each other. Get on with it, Callan told himself again, and dived for the other man's right arm, seeking the place already hurt, but the geezer was as fast as a cat, swerving away from him, using a foot trip that sent Callan spinning into the guard rail of the caisson platform. Frantically he kept on spinning, just missing the

112

follow-up kick that would have killed him, using his momentum to launch himself back at him again, to grunt in agony as a three finger strike just missed its target and smashed into the hard-packed muscle of his shoulder. It was momentum alone that brought him through, and the whole weight of his body slammed on to the other's injured arm, and the man yelled because this was unbearable pain, but went on fighting even so, the left hand seeking to strike again. But the pain had slowed him too much, and Callan grabbed the hand, levered and threw him to the edge of the caisson.

For that kind of fighting, between experts, it was the easiest of throws, and the other man should have done a perfect break-fall and bounced to his feet before Callan could reach him. But the pain defeated him once again: he was still struggling to roll away as the toe of Callan's shoe found the precise spot just below the base of the skull that ends all fights. The last sound he heard in the world was the click of his own spine breaking: after that there was no more pain.

Callan turned him over, frantically seeking the gun. As his hand touched it he was aware of a shadow where before there had been light. He looked up at the biggest Alsatian he had ever seen. In utter silence it had climbed the caisson steps; in utter silence it was looking at him, crouched and ready. The hair round its neck stood up like a ruff, its lips pulled back from teeth like miniature sabres. Callan had seen dogs like this before. They weren't the kind that went round with guard patrols. This one, Callan knew, was a killer. Once he'd done a course with a man who trained them to be just that; a man who had told him, with complete satisfaction in his own achievement, that if one of his dogs ever caught him in a confined space and he had no weapon – then he had no chance either. The dog was always faster, more accurate, more single-minded than a human being could ever hope to be. Suddenly the dog began a growl that was almost inaudible; the great ruff of hair stood up even further and Callan, still watching it, made his hands search the body. The gun was there, in a holster by the pants' waist, the kind with a spring-clip. It was as he was feeling for the release clip that the dog jumped.

It hurled itself at him in a graceful easy leap that must have been beautiful: it was certainly deadly. The dog came at him like a projectile that weighed a hundred pounds at least, its teeth aimed at his throat. Callan hurled himself sideways, bumping against the man he had killed, and the dog's claw clipped open his cheek as it sailed over him and saw the gaping hole of the caisson. For the first time, it howled, in a great bellow of fear, that was cut off short by a softened thud as it hit the concrete below.

Wearily Callan got to his feet, and in the distance another dog barked in answer, then was cut off short. He turned to the dead man, and saw him sliding head-first into the hole. Callan landed across his legs in a flailing dive, then hauled back frantically. The dead man had been solid muscle: it needed all the strength of both arms to hold him, then inch him back to the lip of the hole. What happened then he could see quite clearly. The weight of the body pressed down on the lip as Callan dragged and heaved, and eventually, when it had reached the waist, pressed down on the release mechanism of the holster. As Callan watched, the gun eased forward, butt first. He released the body and grabbed for the gun, but the dead man defeated him, sliding forward into Callan's way as he reached for the gun butt. Man and gun together disappeared into the caisson, and Callan remembered that another dog had barked.

He went down the caisson ladder and ran towards the road, hugging every shadow he could find. But the dog's handler had spotted him, whistled, pointed, and the dog took off after him at once. He risked one look behind him as he ran. The dog was twenty yards away, and gaining on him with each bound. Callan leaped for some scaffolding as the dog finally drew close: its own leap far more powerful than his. He kicked and caught it on the shoulder, but the dog twisted in the air, landed clean, leaped again as Callan ran along a plank bridge to a ladder, the only chance he had, swarming up, chest heaving, muscles ready to crack, but the eyes thank God still working well enough to show him the dog on guard at the ladder's foot, and the thin piece of steel girder that was all the ladder led to.

It was two inches wide, and twenty feet above the ground. Steeplejacks could walk along it as if it was Oxford Street, thought Callan, but not me. He found he was wrong. The dog's handler fired at him, and the bullet hit the girder, ricocheted, wailing, out of sight. Callan mounted it and walked, see-sawing, arms outspread, to the next ladder – and the dog trotted along the plank below him, and was waiting for him when he arrived. The next shot just missed his foot, and he staggered on again, the dog exactly below him. But this time he couldn't make the next ladder. Fear, dizziness, fatigue, brought him up short. There was a vertical upright half way across, and he hung on to it while the dog waited with limitless patience, and Callan decided that he would sooner be shot than face the dog. Two more bullets came, one to ricochet off the upright, inches from his hand, the other through the skirt of his raincoat. The bastard was a marksman all right. He didn't want to shoot him, he wanted him to fall and break his neck, or let the dog finish him off.

Callan felt the raging hate boil inside him. This didn't have even the decency of execution about it: this was filth. He looked across to the next vertical beam. There was a rope dangling near it; a rope that led to a metal hopper as big as a coffin. One more chance he thought – and if the box is empty it'll do for mine. He set off once more, and his faithful friend below went with him. Again he reached the girder, and again hung on. The hopper was suspended six feet above him, but clear of him too, poised exactly above the plank where man's best friend was waiting.

As Callan reached for the rope and pulled, he thought he heard the dog's handler whistle again. If he did he was too late. The hopper's mouth opened, and an avalanche of bricks roared out, the dog disappeared. Callan came down the rope hand over hand, and hit the ground running, making straight for the fence now, swerving as he ran, but there were no more shots. He went over the fence like a gymnast, and came back into a world of streets and street-lights, of cars flashing past, and people inside them who knew nothing of Callan; who would never know whether he lived or died... He felt a sticky warmth on his face, and put a hand to it. Blood. Where the first dog had got him.

He took out a handkerchief and dabbed at it. Have to have it seen to. It would be daft to die of blood-poisoning after all that...

He looked down over the fence. A man in security guard's uniform was pulling at a pile of bricks. One man. But Hunter had said there'd be three of them. Maybe they'd thought two would be enough – or maybe they'd been keeping the third one in reserve, just in case. Callan watched the guard, hauling out bricks, throwing them away. If he'd had a target pistol like that Woodman he'd been trying he could have killed him easy. Suddenly the man uncovered the dog, and his whole body went rigid in a way that at first Callan couldn't explain: and then he realised. He was crying. He'd have been an even easier shot than when he was pulling at the bricks. Look up, you bastard. Let me see your face. But the man in security guard's uniform looked only at the dog, and when he walked away, he never looked back.

Behind Callan the voice said, 'Got a bit lost, have we?'

Callan turned, careful not to make it too fast. The voice had to be a policeman's. It was. Big, even for a copper, and with a mate watching from the wheel of a Panda car.

'Just going home,' said Callan.

The copper's eyes looked at his face.

'We've hurt ourself,' he said.

'Yeah,' said Callan. 'Fell over. I tore my

coat too.' He gestured at the spot where the bullet had gone through it.

'I think we've been fighting,' the copper said.

'Who me? You must be joking,' said Callan, and even the inflection sounded like Lonely.

'And drinking,' said the copper. 'D and D. That's what we are. Drunk and disorderly.'

One Scotch, Callan thought. At Lonely's aunty's. And that was hours ago. But I've been disorderly all right – and that was with experts.

'Honestly,' he said, 'I just had a few drinks, that's all. Only I'm not used to it. That's why I fell over. Please let me go home. The wife'll kill me as it is.'

The copper liked that. Maybe he was henpecked himself.

'Let's see you walk then,' he said, and Callan moved off. The copper said nothing, and he kept on going. Suddenly the Panda car drew up beside him, a window wound down.

'All right,' the copper said. 'Get on back to your struggle – and if she hits us with a frying pan we don't hit her back, right? Otherwise we might see the inside of a nick.'

Callan kept on walking; humbly.

Lonely was not pleased to see him, definitely not. It was late and he'd had a trying day, and anyway he'd been told, over and over he'd been told, that Callan was bad

119

news. And the people who'd told him knew all about bad news. And anyway he'd been asleep. All the same, when Callan stood on his doorstep, he let him in. Mr. Callan knew all about bad news too. Callan looked from the rotting four-poster to the tellys, nodded politely to the Annigoni portrait, then forced open the window. Lonely yelped and grabbed for a dressing-gown.

'Steady on,' he said. 'I'll catch me death.'

Callan looked at him, swathed in scarlet silk. Nicked from a geezer twice his size. He looked like a present from Woolworth's gift-wrapped by Harrods.

'I almost did,' he said.

And of course the smell came. Just as well he'd opened the window.

'Didn't you see your mate then?' Lonely asked.

'He wasn't a mate at all,' said Callan. 'He lied to you Lonely. There's no limit to the low tricks some people get up to.'

'It wasn't my fault,' Lonely said. 'Honest it wasn't.'

He watched as Callan turned towards him; saw the deep scratch on his face.

'You've hurt yourself,' he said.

'No,' Callan said. 'Somebody else did that. Got any whisky?'

Bleeding liberty, said Lonely. Comes in at this hour and expects me to give him Scotch. But he said it to himself.

He poured from a grimy bottle into an almost clean tooth-mug, then watched as Callan first gulped, then sipped, then looked at him.

'Aren't you having any?' Callan asked.

'Mr Callan – it's two in the morning.'

He watched as Callan poured whisky on to his handkerchief, then dabbed cautiously at the scar on his face.

'I do choose my times, don't I?' he said. 'Sorry old son. But I've got to get this seen to.'

'I can't do nothing medical,' said Lonely.

Callan said gravely: 'I wouldn't dream of asking. Only I do need a doctor, you see. One that'll keep his mouth shut, if you follow.'

'I don't know any doctors,' Lonely said. 'Barring the Groper.'

'The Groper?'

'That poof we did bird with. Struck off he was. For interfering.'

'Interfering?'

'With fellers. *You* remember. Used to make lipstick in the paint-shop.'

Suddenly Callan did remember.

'You mean he's still at it?'

'Queer as a nine-pound note,' said Lonely. 'Oh – I see what you mean. He ain't supposed to – but he still gets work. Abortions mostly. Fancy a bird trusting herself to him—'

'Who better?' said Callan. 'Know where he lives?' Lonely nodded. 'On the phone?'

Lonely nodded again. Reluctantly. 'Give him a buzz old son. Tell him he's got a patient.'

'But the phone's on the landing,' Lonely said.

'You've got your dressing-gown.'

'People don't like the noise when it's late.'

'So keep your voice down,' said Callan, then added: 'Keep it down anyway.'

Lonely dragged on his slippers, then moved to the door.

'He'll kill me,' he said.

'No he won't,' said Callan. 'Not if you tell him I've still got my boyish charm.'

When Lonely came back, Callan was pouring another whisky.

'Help yourself, Mr. Callan,' Lonely said.

'I just have,' said Callan. 'Sure you won't have one?'

'All I want's me bed,' said Lonely. 'The Groper says come straight over. Here.' He handed Callan a torn edge of newspaper. 'I've wrote down the address.'

'You're very obliging,' Callan said, and lifted his glass in a toast.

'Confusion to the R.S.P.C.A.' he said, and drank.

'You really didn't get a gun, Mr. Callan?' Lonely asked.

'That's right.'

'So you're still in shtuck then?'

'Right again.'

Lonely gulped. 'You can stay here if you

122

like,' he said at last.

'Thanks old son,' said Callan. 'You've done enough.'

He put the glass down and went to the door.

Lonely said, 'You'll call me if you need anything, won't you?'

Callan turned and looked at him. Fear written all over him, and yet he could still make an offer like that.

'Yeah,' he said. 'I'll do that. Thanks.' He looked again in wonder at the little terrified man. 'You sure you don't mind?'

'Of course not,' said Lonely, stoutly and unconvincingly.

'I never seem to bring you anything but trouble, do I?' Callan said at last.

'You don't want to worry about that, Mr. Callan,' Lonely said. 'You and me are mates.'

9

The Groper lived about ten minutes' walk away, even at the pace that Callan was walking, but his flat was very different from Lonely's. Silk was the first thing you saw: Thai silk the colour of ripe fruits, tangerine, lemon, apricot, plum – on furniture, curtains, walls; in one room even on the ceiling. Nice furniture too; sofas and chairs you could float on, stools covered in gros-point the Groper had embroidered himself, two Beardsley drawings on the walls. The Groper had done well for himself, and for the swinger who'd let him in. A dressing-gown even more gorgeous than Lonely's, and a gold charm bracelet so loaded with charms he had trouble raising his wrist. Pretty too, in an English rose kind of way: like a choirboy on a picture postcard, a sulky choirboy. Here's one queen who doesn't like me, Callan thought. I wonder why? Maybe he's a feller too.

This is hardly the ideal time of night to come bothering the doctor,' the queen said. 'He needs his rest.'

Callan said, 'I know. If it hadn't been an emergency–'

The queen giggled. It was a soft, malicious sound – and utterly feminine.

'An emergency? A teeny scratch like that? Really.'

The Groper came in then, instantly aware of a scene that, Callan was sure, he had played many times before. The fact that he'd taken time to put a suit on didn't seem to reassure the boyfriend in the least.

'Thank you nurse, you may go,' the Groper said. The queen stayed where he was.

'He *says* it's an emergency,' he said. 'That *minute* scratch.'

'There may be more you can't see,' said the Groper.

'I'm sure there are,' said the queen.

'Look sweetheart,' Callan said. 'Do me a favour. Untwist your knickers. The Gro – the doctor and I are old college friends.'

'College?' the queen said. 'You?'

'We can't all be successes in this life,' Callan said.

'How true,' said the Groper. 'Even I have known misfortune in my time. How can I refuse to succour those less fortunate than myself? Do *run along* nurse. If we need you, I'll ring.'

The queen left. Before he slammed the door Callan heard the words, 'Succour indeed.'

The Groper said complacently, 'Nurse is really rather a dish – but *so* jealous.'

125

'With you around he's got reason,' said Callan.

'You always were an old flatterer,' the Groper said. 'Now what have you been up to, dear?'

Callan showed him the scratch, and the Groper turned his face to the light. The touch of his hand was cool, gentle, and quite impersonal.

'Been playing with the nasty rough boys again?' he asked.

'That's right,' said Callan. 'Only this was a nasty rough dog.'

For once the Groper forgot to be camp.

'It must have been a hell of a size,' he said.

'It was.'

The fingers continued to touch his face. 'Was?'

'I regret to tell you that it died,' said Callan.

'Oh don't waste your regrets on me, dear,' the Groper said. 'I've never been one for dogs. Cats now – cats I find enchanting. But perhaps they're not butch enough for you?' He bent, and sniffed at Callan's face. 'What a *curious* aftershave.'

'That's Scotch,' said Callan.

'I bet you wriggled when you put it on,' said the Groper. 'I wish I'd been there.' He moved away then to face Callan.

'I'll clean it up for you a bit more and give you an injection,' he said. 'That's all it needs really. No stitches I mean. You won't have a scar. Pity in a way. You'd look absolutely scrumptious with a scar.'

He opened a drawer, took out a syringe, bottles and cotton wool, and turned back to Callan. The injection was nothing, but the new stuff stung worse than the whisky.

'You always were a brave boy,' the Groper said. 'I wish nurse had been here to see you.'

'Why the hell do you call him nurse?'

'Because he is one. S.R.N. dear.'

'Helps in the business?'

'Invaluable dear. A lovely bedside manner.'

'And business is good?'

'Never better. I thought the Pill would have killed it – but the little darlings forget, bless them, and go straight into the Pudding Club. Then it's off to Aunty Groper and away we go.'

'So this is going to cost me?'

'No dear. This one's on the house.'

'D'you mind if I ask why?'

'When we were in the nick I fancied you. Absolutely avid I was. And you knew it. You never did anything about it, but you never used it against me either.'

'Thanks,' said Callan, then: 'You really happy, Groper?'

'Call no man happy until he is dead. I miss – certain things. I was really good at my job you know. But I really am rather well off and that's such a comfort.'

Callan said, 'I know a feller's having trouble

with his eyes. D'you think you could help him?'

'No,' the Groper said. 'Eyes are specialist business.'

'This feller's got to have an operation—'

'I told you dear. Ophthalmology isn't my line.'

'But in the meantime he needs eyedrops. That's all. It shouldn't be all that difficult.'

'What kind of drops?'

'I could get you some.'

The Groper stooped quickly and looked into Callan's eyes, and Callan cursed himself for being in too much of a hurry.

'Retina,' the Groper said. 'You poor sweetie.' He put his hand under Callan's chin and lifted it to the light.

'You shouldn't play with the nasty rough boys,' he said. 'Really you shouldn't.'

The nurse came in with coffee, and there was shouting and screaming, but at least Callan knew the Groper would help. He even found him a bed to sleep on, when the tumult finally died.

'Beds are no problem here, dear. This is the anti-maternity ward,' he said. 'But you must be up in the morning before the customers arrive. You'd have them wondering what the world's coming to.'

He reached the hospital early, and sat outside, waiting his turn, as they went in one by

128

one. Nobody he wanted to talk to, nothing to read – even if he'd been willing to risk it; all he could do was sit there and think – and worry. One of his would-be executioners was dead, and that was good. But it still left two – and that was as bad as it could be. Two would most likely have taken him even if he had a gun. As it was – he tried to remember what he had seen of the man in the security guard's uniform. Tallish, medium build, and that was it. He'd never even got a look at his bloody face. Fond of dogs, the bastard. Cried when he dug it out dead. He hadn't done any crying when he'd tried to force Callan off the girder... But he had another reason for wanting to kill Callan now. And when he did it, it wouldn't be an easy death. On the other hand the need for revenge might make him careless, and that way – be your age, Callan, he told himself. You're forgetting number three.

They'd set up a good job that first time. Sending 'Judd' to Lonely was a nice touch. And it would have worked too, if Callan hadn't known Judd so well. Hunter was right. Judd was terrified of him. Nothing could make him disobey Hunter's orders. But that aside – they'd set it up well. Guard dogs, for instance. Neat, that was. Clever. Nasty accident. Body of unidentified man. Questions in the House about the use of savage, dangerous animals. Callan wondered what they'd done with the real guard dogs? The ones they'd used on him had been assassins, pros, specially imported for the job, like their masters. The real dogs had probably been fed lumps of steak, with tranquilliser sauce. And the real security guards were probably still wondering what hit them. Teach them a bit about security.

He moved up another place and thought about his next move. It didn't take much brains to realise he didn't have one – not on his own initiative. He could take the count's job and maybe disappear – only he wouldn't. He could do a job on his own – knock off a shop or a garage or something – only he wouldn't. That obstinate honesty was the only value he had left, and he couldn't let it go. The only thing left after that was waiting for them to move – and hoping they'd be careless enough to let him wind up with a gun. He had more chance of winning a football pool. He forced himself to think instead of the friends he had. Aside from the count – and he'd wanted something for himself – he seemed to have two. Both of them first met in the nick, both breaking the law at every chance that offered, and both so bloody vulnerable. The queen and the smeller.

Hunter said, 'They made a try last night.'

'A try?' said Meres. 'They didn't succeed?'

'Far from it,' Hunter said. 'It was something of a fiasco, I'm afraid. Callan killed one of them – and both their dogs.'

Christ, Meres thought. He's actually proud of Callan.

Aloud he said, 'He did that without a gun?'

'Certainly,' said Hunter. 'He's very able you know.' He looked at Meres. 'Dear boy, I know what you're thinking.'

'Do you, sir?'

'That I regret his loss. And so I do. But I shall allow him to go, even so.'

'You're quite sure they'll kill him, sir?'

'Quite sure. Under the circumstances, they can't fail.' He leaned forward at the sofa table, clasped his hands on the empty blotter. The cuffs of his shirt gleamed like icing. 'We get our man from Russia back today,' he said. 'I want you to collect him.'

'But surely, sir–' said Meres.

'Yes?'

'Wasn't the bargain that we didn't get our man back till Callan was dead?'

'No,' Hunter said. 'The bargain was that I should throw Callan out and let their three killers in – or rather that was my part of it. I fulfilled it, and now they've fulfilled their part.'

'Then can't we take Callan back?' asked Meres.

'Cheat them you mean?'

'Yes, sir.'

'My dear Toby – I thought you detested Callan.'

'I do sir. But he's one of ours after all.'

'Just as you are,' said Hunter. 'The point had not escaped me – or you, I gather. Bad for morale, eh Toby? I weighed that factor. It was heavy – but not quite heavy enough.' He leaned back. 'They're flying our chap in via East Germany. Plane from Dresden.' He held out a typewritten slip and a photograph. 'Go and pick him up.'

Meres crossed the room and took them, then looked at the face on the photograph. 'Good God,' he said. 'That's Zhilkov. He's a K.G.B. colonel. I worked on his file two years ago.'

'And last year he went double – and this year they caught him.'

'They must want Callan very badly,' Meres said.

'The thought had not escaped me,' said Hunter. 'Go and fetch him.'

Meres moved to the door.

'Oh by the way, Meres,' Hunter said. 'That girl Susan Marsden. I don't think it will be necessary for you to see her again.'

It was his turn at last, and Nurse Somerset's face showed concern. 'Didn't the drops work?' she asked.

'They were fine for a bit,' said Callan. 'But I got a touch of double vision this morning.

132

It went away after a while, but I thought–'

'You were quite right,' she said, 'but I don't think you'll be able to see the doctor this morning. I'm sorry.'

She sounded sorry, and looked sorry, and Callan regretted lying to her. After the exercise he'd had the night before, he should have had quadruple vision, but so far his eyes had been fine. The first bit of luck he'd had in days.

'Did you do any heavy lifting or anything?'

'No,' he said, and that at least was true. 'Nothing like that. It just sort of happened. Came and went. I thought if you gave me some more drops–'

'It's worth a try,' she said. Callan watched as she went to the table, opened the box that contained the drops. He'd wait around till her lunch-hour, then come in and pick up a couple of samples for the Groper. But even that wasn't necessary. As she took the drops out, the doctor's buzzer sounded and she went into his room. Callan had plenty of time to help himself before she came back again to administer the swimming coolness that left his eyes so clear, until the next time.

'Thanks,' he said.

'You're welcome.'

But she didn't smile. The shyness had come back.

He left her and took a walk. In the hospital grounds birds were singing, and the flowers still outnumbered the weeds. The sun shone fitfully, as if it were out of practice, but when it did shine the warmth bit deep, and Callan walked on out to the street and found a chemist's shop, and bought a pair of sunglasses. No point in taking chances. He put them on in the shop and looked at his face in a mirror.

'My God,' he thought. 'All I need now's a white stick.'

But the sun felt good, and the Groper's bed had been soft enough to sleep in. He walked to the park where children were playing, the very small children who were too young for school; tottering across the grass as he'd tottered on a girder, finding cause for wonder in a flower, a pebble, a leaf, while their mums stabbed at their knitting and talked about bingo. He remembered the girl who'd said she'd wait for him when he went in the Scrubs. When he came out she'd been pushing a pram. Probably pushed a couple more since then, but none of the kids in them had been his. His was an adult world: he'd forgotten how kids behaved, almost he'd forgotten what they looked like; that grave intentness, the sudden onset of rage, or tears. He'd have liked to have kids, he thought, but not while he was doing the job he did. Kids, a wife, even a steady girl-friend; it wasn't on. He'd known section operatives who'd married, and wondered what lies they told. Wondered how they could stand it come to that. Better on your own really. And nobody was more alone than he was. Parents knocked off in the blitz, and the aunty who'd brought him up, dead years ago. He'd cried for her then, when he got the letter in Malaya, but at least she never knew he'd been in the nick.

10

Lunchtime came near, and he left the park as the prams were filling, and strolled back the way he had come to the pub he wanted. Nothing like the 'Greyhound' this one. Old wooden counter, beer in glass mugs, and a choice of hot pies, sausage and mash and bread and cheese. Callan chose the sausage and mash, on the barmaid's advice. 'Always good they are dear.' He tried a mouthful, and decided her taste-buds must have exploded. Still it was fuel, and the beer was good.

She came in far more at ease this time. This was her pub, where people knew her, accepted her, and went on about their own affairs. She ordered a shandy and a sandwich, and even agreed with the barmaid that the weather had turned out marvellous. And then she saw Callan. He went on eating, but waved to her, and at last she came over to him. Reluctantly, but she came. He stood up, then moved over to let her sit beside him.

'What a coincidence,' she said.

'Not really,' said Callan. 'You told me you ate at the pub round the corner. I went round all the corners, but there's only the one pub.'

'I told you it was always full of hospital people.'

'And you don't like them to see you eating with a patient?'

'To you I must sound very foolish,' she said.

'Everyone's foolish sometimes,' said Callan. 'Even me. I ordered the sausage and mash.'

Her laughter, he thought, was the sort of reward you could break a leg trying to earn.

'Reading today?' he asked.

'I told you I always do.'

'What?' She looked at him, questioning. 'What d'you read, I mean?'

'History,' she said. 'Politics, Economics, Sociology. Does it sound boring?'

'It sounds as if it could be.'

'It is boring,' she said. 'So many important things are. Do you read – when your eyes are all right, I mean?'

'Yeah,' he said. 'Military history.'

'Nothing else?' He shook his head. 'Always wars?'

'Not wars,' he said. 'Battles. The men who fought them – Hannibal, Caesar, Wellington, Lee – blokes like that. I like figuring out why they won – and lost.'

'I think war is disgusting,' she said.

'I agree with you,' said Callan. 'And I've been in one. That's why I like to treat battles as an academic study – like the slave trade in one of your economics books.'

She winced at that, but the laughter came at last.

'I asked for that,' she said. 'I seem to have an unfortunate habit of being rude to you. I'm sorry.'

'A lot of people do,' said Callan. 'Mostly they don't apologise.'

'What war were you in?'

'Malaya,' he said.

'Fighting the Chinese guerrillas?'

'That's right.'

As he watched, he could see another question forming, but it didn't come. She finished her sandwich and her shandy, then rose to her feet.

'I must go,' she said, and Callan swallowed his beer.

'I'll come with you,' he said.

'There's no need.'

'You be the judge of your needs,' said Callan, 'and I'll be the judge of mine.'

He didn't take her arm until they had left the pub, but then he steered her towards the park.

'It's miles out of the way,' she said.

'And the sun is shining. You can catch up with your reading when it rains.'

They walked down a path across grassland now deserted by children. This was the lovers' hour, and the couples embraced, oblivious, intent, aware only of the warmth and closeness of another human being. Again she stiffened beside him, but he walked on un-hurried, and made no move to leave the path.

'The sun makes you homesick?' he asked.

'Sometimes,' she said. 'But it has to be hotter than this.'

Then he asked more questions, and she found herself answering them, the words pouring out faster and faster, about her home, her parents, her present loneliness, till at last the whole lunch hour was up and she had to run to the hospital, and as she ran tell herself that she must not, must not be drawn to this man, and the next second wonder how long it would be before he came again to see her.

He'd got Lonely to pick up Meres' suitcase and leave it at Aunty Glad's. At least he could have a change of underwear while he tried to figure out what their next move would he. The route he took to Chelsea would have horrified a time and motion man, but it made sense to Callan. He knew he wasn't being followed. He pressed the button labelled de Courcy Mannering, confessed that he was Callan, and was, at last, admitted. She wore another cashmere twin-set. No pearls this time, but a diamond on her finger that made him want to put on his sunglasses.

'Lonely brought your suitcase,' she said. 'I'd be obliged if you wouldn't use my home as a left-luggage office.'

'I thought you were doing the Count a favour?' said Callan.

'Favours yes,' said Aunty Glad. 'Bloody liberties, no.'

'My case is a bloody liberty?'

'I'm known here,' Aunty Glad said, 'as *Miss* de Courcy Mannering. Any strange gentleman's luggage is a bloody liberty.'

And Callan realised that she wasn't fooling.

'All right,' he said, 'just give me time for a wash and a change and I'll shift it.'

'You're very obliging,' said Aunty Glad.

When he came back she'd even poured a drink for him. He looked at the suitcase; good leather, polished, steel-frame, and almost empty. It seemed a shame to waste a good case like that. He asked Aunty Glad for a carrier-bag, and she showed no surprise at all when he transferred the suitcase's contents to it.

'Going to visit your uncle?' she asked. Callan nodded. 'Don't take a penny less than five quid,' she said. 'That's real hide.'

Callan thanked her, and asked, humbly, if he might use the phone. After he had promised faithfully that it was a local call he was told that he could. She left him, and he dialled the Groper, and Nurse's voice said, 'Hullo?'

'This is the man who got his face

scratched,' Callan said. 'Let me speak to the boss.'

'I really don't know if he's available at the moment.'

'You'd better find out,' said Callan, 'or I'll come over and scratch *your* face.'

The Groper came on the line.

'I wish you wouldn't upset nurse,' he said.

'I wish he wouldn't upset me,' said Callan. 'I got the drops.'

'Read it to me.'

Callan read it: maker's name, laboratory address, the complex – and to him meaningless – chemical formula.

When he had finished, the Groper said, 'It's only a palliative you know. Not a cure.' There was a pause, then he added, 'You need surgery dear.'

'I'll be getting it,' said Callan. 'But there's a waiting list. In the meantime I need the drops.'

'I'll get them for you,' the Groper said. 'It might take a couple of days – but they won't cure you, you know.'

'I've been told,' said Callan.

'And there's another thing,' the Groper said. 'You can't put them in yourself – and Lonely's hardly a trained nurse, is he? You'd have to go to someone who knows what he's doing.'

'You know what you're doing,' said Callan.

The Groper sighed.

'Very well,' he said. 'I'll put them in for you.'

'Thanks, Groper,' said Callan.

'But they still won't cure you.'

Next was the problem of Meres' suitcase. The best offer he could get was three pounds fifty, but by that time he was sick of lugging the damn thing around from pawnbroker to pawnbroker. He took it. Next time he needed to pawn anything, he thought, he would take Lonely's Aunty Glad with him. In the meantime he would buy her nephew a drink... He phoned the necessary pubs, caught him at the third one, and arranged to meet in another that Lonely never used. 'Make sure you're not followed,' said Callan, and Lonely said he would. That was enough for Callan. The little man could disappear down a crack in the pavement.

The pub Callan chose was more renowned for its beer than its elegance, and that suited Lonely. He knocked off a pint while Callan was still sipping his first Scotch. Callan said, 'It beats me where you put it.'

Lonely grinned; Callan's voice was admiring.

'Maybe it's because I worry a lot,' Lonely said.

Callan thought: The poor little perisher thinks he's joking, as Lonely signalled for the same again. When they arrived, Callan paid.

Lonely said, 'Sure you can manage it, Mr. Callan?'

'I'm sure,' said Callan. Lonely looked at the carrier-bag.

'I see you're not carrying that posh suitcase.'

'Oh yes I am,' said Callan, and showed him three pound notes.

'Things really are bad, aren't they?' said Lonely.

'They'll get better,' said Callan.

'Course they will,' Lonely said. 'I know how it is with you class operators. You can't touch small jobs when you're skint. It's bad for your reputation.'

You'd think I was a bleeding film star, thought Callan.

'How's your Aunty Gertie?' Callan asked.

'All right,' Lonely swallowed more beer.

'Doesn't like me, does she?'

'I keep telling her we're mates,' said Lonely, 'and she keeps telling me I'm her nephew. If she bought an electric dish-washer that'd be a nephew an' all.'

'She's looking out for you,' said Callan. 'She thinks I'm trouble. I don't blame her.'

'So does Aunty Glad think you're trouble,' said Lonely. It doesn't stop her letting you in.'

'I thought she liked me,' said Callan.

'That's right, she does,' said Lonely. 'But that doesn't mean she'd *help* you. There's only one person in the world Aunty Glad would go out of her way to help – and that's Aunty Glad.'

'So why's she doing it? Because the Count asked her?'

'Because the Count made her, if you ask me,' said Lonely.

'I am asking you,' said Callan. 'How could he make her? I thought she was retired?'

'So she is,' said Lonely. 'But the Count – nobody ever retires from him. You must know what he's like.'

Well enough, thought Callan. I once thought I'd have to kill him. But he didn't say it aloud. To reduce Lonely to terror would be neither friendly nor charitable. 'I know what he's like,' he said.

'Well there you are then,' said Lonely. 'You must have done him a big favour for him to go to all that trouble for you.'

I let him live.

'He thinks it's a favour,' said Callan. 'Me – I'm not so sure.'

Lonely gulped more beer. 'Time I bought one,' he said, and went to the bar.

Callan thought about loyalty and obligation. Lonely acknowledged both of them – to Callan. Aunty Gertie, it was clear, knew all about them too, and lavished them on Lonely. Callan himself had suffered from them both: in fact they had almost killed him. Only his had been to an entity – the Section. Not Hunter, not Meres, not Judd, nor any of the others. It was the group itself that had commanded his loyalty, and his obligation: given him a sense of direction, a sense of purpose, and of belonging, when he'd desperately needed all three. Like the army, in the old days – Wellington's time. The scum of the earth who joined only for drink. But the regiment turned out to be father and mother and home to them. And even scum could be grateful for that, and were. It was the regiment they died for. But then their regiments hadn't rejected them, taken their guns away and allowed the enemy to use them for target practice... Enough of that Callan. Think about Aunty Glad, whose sense of loyalty and obligation is only to herself. And she'll help you – and Aunty Gertie won't. Think about Komorowski, who's been a crook for more than twenty-five years and has no sense of loyalty and obligation at all, only a few remaining shreds of a concept called honour that his father knew all about because his father commanded a cavalry regiment... Lonely came back with more booze.

'Cheers,' said Callan, and Lonely didn't so much drink his beer as inhale it.

'You must be one of the original Sons of Suction,' said Callan, and Lonely loved it. 'You know, I've been thinking–'

'Yes, Mr. Callan?'

145

Callan dreaded speaking the next words, and yet they had to be said.

'You've been good to me, Lonely. You've done your best and I'm grateful–'

'I never got you a gun.'

'Not your fault,' said Callan. 'Nobody can get me a gun.' Not even me, he thought, though I came bloody near it. 'But your Aunty Gertie's right. I *am* bad news. Maybe I should keep out of your way for a bit.'

Lonely looked at him, appalled. 'Mr Callan I *tried*,' he said. 'Honest I did.'

'I know that. It's just that–'

'Me two best suppliers. Me very best. I begged them, Mr. Callan.'

'Lonely, I believe you,' Callan said. 'All I'm saying is–'

'And after all that you're telling me you're not my mate any more. Well all I can say is it's bleeding unfair. I fed you, didn't I? I gave you a kip. Go on. Deny it if you can.'

'I'm not denying it,' said Callan. 'I–'

'Bloody snobbery that's all it is,' said Lonely. 'Just because you pull bigger jobs than I do–'

'Will you for Gawd's sake belt up?' Callan said savagely. The little man's voice died as if Callan had chopped him across the throat, and Callan cursed himself. 'I'm sorry old son,' he said. Lonely made no answer.

'Look,' said Callan, 'it's *because* we're mates I'm suggesting this. You know the kind of

146

people I get up against. You could get hurt, son. What kind of a mate would I be if I let that happen?'

'You think I haven't thought about it?' said Lonely. 'But what kind of a mate would I be if I ran away now?'

Callan found that he had no words to answer such a question.

At last he said, 'I'm grateful for that, Lonely. Believe me. And I'm accepting it. We'll keep in touch. Only I don't think we should take any chances with other people.'

'What other people, Mr. Callan?'

'Your Aunty Glad,' said Callan. 'We don't want her hurt, do we?'

There were limits to Lonely's sense of loyalty and obligation.

'Do her good,' he said.

'All the same I think we'll try to leave her out of it,' said Callan. 'Look son, this is how we'll play it. Tonight I'll get a kip somewhere, and tomorrow I'll phone you at a pub – like I did tonight. You tell me which pub you'll be in at six – and I'll call you there. We'll do that every day, only we'll keep switching pubs and times so if anyone did try to follow you we'd make it harder for them. Right?'

'Right,' said Lonely, and Callan had no worries. Lonely had been practising that kind of security since he'd first whizzed sweets out of Woolworth's. 'Where you going to kip, Mr. Callan?' Lonely asked.

'I think I'll keep that one to myself,' said Callan. 'If you don't know, then nobody's going to be able to make you tell, are they?'

The smell came then, but for once Lonely didn't seem to notice it. He was too busy trying to concentrate on keeping his hand steady while he drank.

'You still want me to call you tomorrow?' Callan asked, and Lonely nodded, not trusting himself to speak.

'Right,' said Callan. 'Let's decide on a pub where I can call you.'

And after that, he thought, I'll be off to a doss-house... Another good reason for not telling Lonely. It would be bad for my image.

11

That night he dreamed about Lebichev. That had been one of the early jobs, the ones that had happened before he'd started asking questions and getting involved with his victims; the early days when a job was just an extension of training, and the training had put a final gloss on an instinct for killing that had delighted his tutors, because Callan had from the first been far and away the best pupil they'd ever had. As one of them told Hunter later, 'Even before he came to us Callan could have taken the best men you've got.' It had something to do with reflexes, and more with the kind of nervous courage that, once it has calculated the odds, will follow through to the end, and never forget that survival is always to be welcomed, but never a pre-requisite. A hard body, and a mind of surprising quickness also helped, as did his own particular brand of patience; the patience of a hunting animal that will wait immobile for hours then gamble everything on one destroying blow.

It had been like that with Lebichev, cultural attaché to their London embassy, full of stories about Mayakovski and what his father had told Maxim Gorki; the man who could always get you tickets for the Bolshoi, or the Red Army choir, or Moscow Dynamos, whenever they came over on a visit. The life and soul of every embassy party, Lebichev had been, the good-time Charlie of Millionaires' Row. And he'd looked the part, too. Good-looking in a plump and cuddly way that turned the birds on every time, witty and fluent in his almost unaccented English, hands deftly busy as they offered the caviar, or opened just one more bottle of cold Crimean wine. Everybody loved him, everybody went to him, and quite a lot of people told him their troubles; he was so sympathetic, so understanding, and sometimes he could be so helpful. Money, drugs, an abortion; if you needed it, Lebichev would get it for you; only one day there'd be a knock on the door and you'd find out the hard way that whatever Lebichev got for you had to be paid for.

Not to him. Lebichev was too clever for that. That was why he had such a good run before Hunter finally tracked him down. It was always somebody else who arrived and broke the news that they knew all about you – and that soon everybody else would know all about you too, unless you preferred to do some simple little thing like pass on information, or put a set of trade figures on microfilm, or give a list of exactly which generals from which countries had been present at those last NATO defence talks. And if you didn't – well, the choice was yours, but Lebichev's information would be used, you could rely on that, and the chances were it would ruin you.

But Hunter had got on to him at last, just as Lebichev had got a bite from the biggest fish he'd ever angled for: the daughter of an air-marshal, hooked on drugs, and daddy's darling, who suddenly discovered that the kind of drugs she'd moved on to weren't all that easy to get, until dear, sweet Lebikins came to the rescue. But even he had to go to Paris to arrange a supply of the stuff she needed, and Callan had gone to Paris too, and washed his hands at Orly airport, and never even looked at the man who washed his hands at the next basin, and went off with Callan's briefcase and left his own in exchange... Callan took it to the small, shabby hotel in the Boulevard St. Michel that had been booked for him, checked his room for bugs exactly as he had been taught, then opened the briefcase. A pile of papers, and beneath them, a Smith and Wesson Magnum .38, the webbing harness he preferred, six rounds of ammo, and a silencer that wouldn't even last six rounds. But it would handle three, and if he had to fire more than three he might as well start using artillery. He checked the gun, cleaned it, then put on the harness and practised drawing: not that he intended pulling the gun – the harness wouldn't take the silencer anyway – but practice was what made perfect, and perfect was what he had to be if he was going to do jobs like this one: because Lebichev was a K.G.B. major, executive trained. That meant he'd been taught to handle what they called 'wet jobs': which meant muggings, hi-jackings, murder. And if Lebichev had reached executive grade, then he was good, cuddly charm or no cuddly charm.

He'd never been to Paris before, and he'd never gone back since. One night in Gay Paree, and he'd never seen the Crazy Horse Saloon, not even the Folies Bergère. All he'd done was walk to the Rue Georges Cinq by the route they'd taught him, and that took bloody hours. He carried the briefcase, which contained letters and accounts for a Midlands wholesale firm that was thinking of importing French canned goods, and a card that said he was the manager of their Food and Drink department, just in case. He walked briskly, but not too fast, timing his arrival for the hour Hunter had given him, and was careful not to bump into his fellow pedestrians, particularly with his gun.

He reached the hotel that was far better than his, and took the lift to the floor above Lebichev's, walked down one flight, knocked twice, got no answer, and let himself in with

152

the kind of key not even the best hotels supply. He checked Lebichev's suite carefully, and looked for a place to hide. Hunter had suggested the bathroom, but that was barmy. The bathroom door was opened just enough for a mirror to show exactly who was inside it, and Lebichev hadn't done that by accident. Behind the curtains would have been a good idea if the curtains had been long enough, but they weren't. He settled at last for behind the sofa, and crouched down behind it like someone caught in the act in a French farce, then took out the magnum and fitted on the silencer. Nothing to do but wait, and make sure his joints didn't get stiff...

He waited nearly an hour before he heard the footsteps outside the door, the grate of the key in the lock. Carefully, head lowered, he knelt behind the settee as the door opened and he listened for voices. Hunter had sworn Lebichev would be alone, but Hunter wasn't in his hotel suite. But Hunter had been right, and Callan waited, motionless, scarcely breathing as Lebichev checked his room from the doorway and then at last – oh thank Christ! – shut the door and walked towards the bathroom. Callan stood up behind him and could have sworn he made no sound, but Lebichev whirled round even so – he was that good – his hand grabbing for a gun, and Callan shot him, in the heart, the silencer plopped, and Lebichev's hand pulled reflexively, his gun came out, and Callan shot him again in the head. Two seconds, maybe three, and Lebichev was dead.

Callan went over to him, knelt by his side. A hole in the forehead, a hole in the hand-made suit, and neither much bigger than a cigarette burn; that was what magnums were for. But both bullets had gone right through him. Magnums were for that, too. Callan's gloved hands searched the body. The stuff was there right enough: in the right hand inside pocket. He took it out and left it by Lebichev's left hand, then it was time to go, not rushing, remembering to lock the door, then walk down the stairs and go straight to the public phones, dial the number they'd taught him, ask for the man they'd told him would be there, deliver the message he'd memorised, and hang up, stroll out of the hotel to the corner for the Citroen taxi Hunter had promised would be waiting, check its number and get in. When he paid it off at Orly the gun, harness and silencer were under its back seat, and all he'd left behind was an over-night bag, that contained nothing, not even fingerprints. On the plane going back he drank Scotch, but there was no point in buying a bottle; he hadn't been away long enough to claim a duty-free allowance...

He dreamed the whole thing through,

sequence by sequence, as if he were watching himself in a movie, right up to the part where Hunter had told him what a good job he had done. He had, too. The man he had phoned was an inspector in the Narcotics Bureau and he'd gone straight to Lebichev's hotel and found him, and the drugs. The scandal that caused had lasted for months... A good job, and he hadn't put a foot wrong, so why did he wake up sweating now? He hadn't sweated at the time. Because by now the K.G.B. knew he'd killed Lebichev, and they didn't like it. They liked the scandal even less, and the time had come when he would pay for both.

He lay in one of the row of beds – 'clean accommodation for working men' – the only one who could no longer escape into sleep. On either side of him men moaned, snored, sighed: one whimpered softly, another murmured the same incomprehensible phrase over and over. But only he lay alone in the dark, and remembered how Lebichev had lain after two neat holes had punched the life out of him, how Hunter had gone to see the Air Marshal and taken Callan with him. What Hunter had said had brought first incredulity, then rage, and then at last a crushing realisation of its truth that Callan had found unbearable. And then the girl had come in, the sound of Lebichev's name acting like a magnet even after he was dead, and Callan had watched in stolid silence as her father had pulled back a sleeve of her dress and found the evidence Hunter had promised him was there. Then he hit her. Two months later she was dead. Blood-poisoning from a dirty needle. Sad, stupid, useless; the whole thing. She'd looked a bit like Susan Marsden, he remembered; the same look they all have when they first realise that they've started something that's too big to stop. Maybe Lebichev should have looked like that too, but he hadn't. The expression on Lebichev's face had been one of surprise that the thing that couldn't possibly happen was finally happening. And even though I know, thought Callan, I'll probably look like that too... Susan Marsden, the Air Marshal's daughter. Keeping them supplied was what Komorowski had called the stupidity business. It was a business he knew well, and he was right.

He got up early – the clean accommodation for working men wasn't exactly spotless – bathed and shaved at a public baths, sat in another park, watched other children and mums. It was another day of fitful sunshine. He put on his sunglasses, and the heat, warming his bones, brought his mind back to Komorowski. A life in the sun, plenty of birds and booze; top man until he met somebody better – and only the Susan Marsdens to worry about till it happened. It wasn't on.

But warmth and the thought of girls made him think of Nurse Somerset: grave, attentive, concerned about her reading. A body like that, and all she cared about was her mind. Maybe she thought her mind couldn't hurt her. One day she'd find out how wrong she was... The sun's heat soothed him and he dozed, dreaming of women. No sequences this time, just pictures like portraits: Susan Marsden, Nurse Somerset, the Air Marshal's daughter, Aunty Glad – and a prize if you could spot the link. Something in a box. But Callan couldn't spot the link, and the box wouldn't open. He woke to the chant of children singing, a group of four year olds, intent and serious as cherubim hovering over the crib: Georgie Best, they sang.

Georgie Best, superstar
Walks like a woman and wears a bra–

Then they scattered before their mothers' wrath, and there was laughter in the shrieks their voices made. There would be no laughter, Callan thought, if my killers found me here. Since I've killed one of them already, they won't take any chances. They'd kill me here with those kids watching. You selfish bastard, Callan. Why don't you keep away from children? He got up and walked again, bought a bacon sandwich and tea at a snack bar, then walked on till it was time to call

157

Lonely; let his mate know he'd survived another night.

The little man picked the phone up so fast he must have been sitting right beside it. 'Mister Ca–' he began.

Callan said, 'Don't say my name.'

'I've got to talk to you,' said Lonely.

'Talk then.'

'Not here,' Lonely said. 'It's – confidential.'

'Trouble?' asked Callan.

'My Gawd,' said Lonely.

'The Round Pond, Kensington,' said Callan. 'Go there and have a look at the boats– And stand there by yourself, old son. I want to see you on your own.'

'You know I wouldn't do that to you,' said Lonely.

'Yes son, I know you wouldn't,' said Callan. 'But I know the ones who would, too.'

He took a bus then, up to Hyde Park Corner, Knightsbridge, Kensington Gore, past the rich and sumptuous shops, the solid blocks of houses and flats that used money for foundation stones, to the Albert Hall, incredible as ever. He left the bus and crossed to the Albert Memorial, equally defying belief in its green and shady setting, then walked into the park till he found what he wanted, a screen of trees overlooking the water. On a weekday you didn't expect too many, and he'd guessed it right. A few kids, some of them with nannies, and the kind of sailing boats that took half an hour to cross the pond, and here and there an elderly fanatic with an exact scale model of the Queen Mary or whatever it was, that could do the same trip in a minute and a half. No Lonely, and that was good. Callan wanted to watch him arrive.

He came scuttling along the path five minutes later, raincoat flapping, cloth cap pulled down across his eyes as if sunlight were a disease and he might catch it. When he reached the pond he stood with his back to Callan, as far away from anybody else as he could manage, and Callan watched the path. A minute, two minutes went by, and nobody followed. Lonely stood alone among the well-heeled kids and captains of liners four feet long; about as inconspicuous as a sparrow in a cage full of budgerigars. Callan moved soundlessly across the path to the edge of the pond.

'Hallo,' he said, and Lonely shot up inside his raincoat like toothpaste squeezed in a tube. Callan had known it would happen, it always did – and he could never resist it.

'I wish you wouldn't do that, Mr. Callan,' said Lonely. But that too was part of the ritual.

Callan said, 'Let's walk a bit,' and they strolled away from the wasp-buzz of engines, the shouts of children.

Callan said at last, 'Let's have it.'

'It's the Groper,' said Lonely.

'What about him?'

'That's just it,' said Lonely. 'He wouldn't tell me. But he's in a terrible state, Mr. Callan.'

Callan said, 'Let's have it in order, old son.'

'He rang me up just before I went off to me aunty's–' Lonely looked at Callan's face and added hastily – 'Aunty Gertie's, I mean. The dish washing job. He says he's got to see you. Crying he was – like hysterical and that. I tell him I don't know where you are and he won't wear it. So I tell him I got to go to work and I hang up.'

'And that's it?' Callan asked.

Lonely said, 'I should be so lucky. Somehow he finds out where I'm working and comes over to me aunty's. Carrying on something shocking he was. Keeps saying he's got to see you.'

'Did he use my name?'

'Over and over,' said Lonely. 'I couldn't stop him, Mr. Callan.'

Callan said, 'I believe you. Anyway, I don't suppose it matters. Not any more. Go on.'

'Then he tried to hit me,' said Lonely, 'only me Aunty Gertie's there and she says she'll let him have a mug of tea in the kisser if he puts a finger on me, and he starts crying worse than ever, and I say I'll try to get a message to you and Aunty Gertie tells him to piss off.'

'And what happened then?'

'He pissed off,' said Lonely. 'People always do when Aunty Gertie tells them.'

'So that was the end of it?'

'End?' said Lonely. 'She hadn't even started. "What a bloody disgrace, I was bringing poofs to her place and wasting time when I should have been washing cups, and what did I expect anyway, going mates with a"' – he broke off.

'Bastard like me,' said Callan. 'I really don't bring you much luck do I?'

'All the luck I can handle,' said Lonely. 'And all of it bad. Then she told me to promise never to see you again.'

'And what did you do?'

'I promised never to see you again,' said Lonely. 'Only I crossed my fingers– She was that mad she forgot to look. You know,' he said, in a burst of candour, 'it's the first time I ever did anything me Aunty Gertie told me not to. I'm enjoying it.'

'Where's the Groper now?' Callan asked.

'At his gaff. In his bed by the look of him. Mr. Callan, he looked awful. You going over?'

'No,' said Callan. 'I'll see him. But not at his place. Can you go and tell him to come here?'

'If I go now,' said Lonely. 'Very strict about my lunch hour Aunty Gertie is.'

'Off you go then,' said Callan, 'and mind

you get him on his own before you tell him where I am. Better still – ask him to step outside before you tell him. Right?'

'Just as you say, Mr. Callan.'

He went off at once, and without question. Lonely's was not a questioning mind, and it would have alarmed him to know that Callan was considering the possibility that the Groper's flat might be bugged. Come to that, Callan thought, it alarms me. And even taking the Groper outside wouldn't make him absolutely secure. With the scoop mikes they've got nowadays they could pick one voice out of rush-hour traffic in Regent Street. But scoop-mikes took time to set up, and whatever had been done to the Groper had been done in a hurry. Getting him outside at least increased Callan's chances.

He waited once more in the shelter of the trees, inducing patience by an act of will. There was no point in worrying what the Groper *might* tell him. What he had to do was save his energy, and his adrenalin, for what the Groper *would* tell him, so he sat and waited, and watched the Round Pond Navy, till the Groper swept along the path in a stride that was energetic yet mincing, like the Groper himself. Callan waited while he positioned himself, in view of the trees, then turned his attention to the path, for a minute, two, three, four. Somehow they'd reached the Groper; it wouldn't do to take chances. And while he watched the Groper moved restlessly up and down, looked at his watch, shied away from children. After four minutes Callan left the shelter of the trees and headed to him. He was vulnerable now, totally at risk, but what the Groper had to tell him might justify it, and anyway he'd earned the right to talk to him again, so Callan broke cover and walked briskly to him, aware of every detail of grass and pond and sky, and even more aware of the trees where a man with a gun might hide and choose his shot – and kill.

The Groper saw him at last and couldn't wait. The Round Pond Mariners, some amused, some indignant, all scornful, watched as he ran from the Pond towards Callan, then went back to their ships.

My God, Callan thought. Lonely was right. He really does look ghastly. Fear and shock had aged him with an effectiveness that showed how intense that fear and shock had been. He should have been in bed, under sedation, not running about like a maniac. But then if it comes to that I should be home at my flat, taking it easy, waiting for my operation... The Groper stopped, facing him, and Callan waited. The man seemed absolutely bewildered. His hands became fists, as if he would attack Callan, then opened in a gesture that was almost imploring. His mouth worked, but whether to make words or bellow with grief it was impossible to tell. When he fought to achieve control it was a bitter struggle.

'I – I had to see you,' he said at last.

'I'm here,' said Callan.

'I was going to help you.' There was horror and amazement in his voice. 'We talked, after all those years, and I remembered and I was going to help you.'

'You were going to give me the treatment with the eye-drops,' Callan said.

'That's all off.' He glared at Callan as if he had committed an unforgivable stupidity. 'Surely to God you must see that. After what's happened–'

Callan said, 'But I don't know what's happened.'

'Terry,' the Groper said.

'Terry?'

'Terry Locket,' the Groper said. 'We used to call her Lucy at parties. The boy who lived with me.'

'You called him nurse,' Callan said. 'He didn't like me.'

'God knows he had no reason to.'

The Groper sat, abruptly, as if his legs had given way beneath him, and began tearing up handfuls of grass. Callan sat more slowly, facing him, still watching the path.

'You better tell me,' he said gently. 'It's the only thing that'll do any good.'

'You phoned me,' the Groper said. 'About

the drops.'

'I remember.'

'I got on to a – a business acquaintance of mine who could get them for you. It might take a couple of days, he said. I told him to get them anyway. And then Terry and I had dinner. There was nobody in the clinic and we were rather gay, only he had to go out later. He's got this ghastly old mother in Hammersmith but I make him go and see her because he frets if he doesn't, and Terry's absolute hell when he frets. I – I expected him back by midnight. He didn't come.' He plucked another handful of grass, crushed and twisted it in his fingers.

'Don't stop now,' said Callan. 'Finish it.'

'They – they brought him back at two in the morning,' the Groper said.

'They?'

'Two men. Two great big he-men just like you. They'd been having a little fun with Terry. A little *fun.*'

He put his hands to his face then, weeping into the matted grass.

'Crying won't help him,' Callan said.

The Groper's hands dropped then. Hands and face alike were stained with green. 'You bitch,' he said.

'How badly did they beat him?' Callan asked.

'No,' the Groper said. 'Not a beating.'

'What then?'

165

'Remember when you came to see me about that scratch on your face? You remember I dressed it for you?'

'I remember,' said Callan.

'I said you would look absolutely scrumptious with a scar on your face.'

'That's right.'

'Terry won't look scrumptious at all,' said the Groper. 'Of course he's got rather more than one scar. More like a dozen. They must have used a scalpel – or a razor. I don't think it would be possible to make a knife as sharp as that.' He looked at Callan. 'You don't say anything. Don't you think something ought to be said?'

'Finish it,' said Callan. 'Then I'll speak.'

'They'd gone deep,' the Groper said. 'There were places where the flesh was hanging– Even with stitches he–' His hands moved up again, but he stopped them before they reached his face, and this time there was nothing but hatred in his eyes for Callan and all his world. 'I suppose this must be the merest commonplace to you.'

'I've seen it,' Callan said. 'But I've never done it.'

'I covered his face and called the hospital,' the Groper said. 'They had an ambulance with me in minutes. They might as well have taken days.'

'Terry died?'

'Oh no. He'll live. If you can call it living.

Then we had police and statements, and all that.'

'Did you tell them who did it?'

'I don't know who did it,' the Groper said. 'They think it's sadists who don't like queers. They could be right.'

'The two men,' said Callan. 'When did they leave?'

'After they'd shown me Terry.'

'You described them to the police?'

'I couldn't,' the Groper said. 'Even if I'd had the nerve. They wore masks.'

'Did you say you'd seen them?' The Groper shook his head. 'Did Terry?'

'I – I said he rang the bell and I found him unconscious on the door-step. Terry said they grabbed him on his way home and took him in a car to some waste ground or other. Then they – started to cut him. One held him; the other cut. Very careful, he said. Like a surgeon. When they grabbed him their faces were muffled and just before they cut him, they put on the masks. They even wore overalls – so the blood wouldn't mark their suits.' He paused, then said, 'Surely it's your turn to say something now.'

Callan said, 'You haven't finished.'

'How much more of his blood do you want?'

'The two men talked about me,' said Callan. 'I want you to tell me what they said.'

'They knew about the eye-drops,' the

Groper said. 'Knew you'd asked for them, knew I'd said I'd get them. They – said I wasn't to help you; that if I did I'd wind up looking worse than Terry.'

'And that's why they did it?'

'That's why. Like men with no feelings. Not even anger. Not even hate. As if they'd had surgery, and all the feelings had been removed. They told it all twice because one of them said I'd been upset and I mightn't have understood it the first time, so they went through it all again. They were – very patient. I think that was the most frightening thing of all.'

'Did they have any kind of accent?'

The Groper said wearily, 'My dear, they could have had two heads apiece and I don't think I'd have noticed.' Then he stopped for a moment, and thought. 'No, no accent that I could remember. No accent at all.'

'Did they tell you to come and see me?'

'No.'

'You're taking a terrible risk,' said Callan. 'Why?'

'Because I'm a silly old queen,' said the Groper. 'I had to see you. I – didn't love Terry you know. I don't think queens do love very much, not the way straight people do. Most of the gay crowd I've ever met have been as lecherous as monkeys. But he was nice and reliable and hardworking, and we enjoyed our jolly romps together, even if

168

we did have our little bits on the side.'

'I think he was in love with you,' said Callan, 'if jealousy's anything to go by.'

'You always were an outspoken boy,' the Groper said. 'Even in the nick. It isn't always a virtue you know. Can't you see – if Terry loves me, that makes it worse.'

'Who for?' said Callan, and the Groper flinched.

'For both of us. But it'll be worse for him. It'll make me feel more responsible – for a while, but in the end I'll leave him. I'll tell us both I won't, but I know I will – because he won't be pretty any more.'

Callan said, 'I think this time you'll surprise yourself.'

'I did fall in love once,' the Groper said. 'In the nick. I fell in love with you. Very pure, my love for you. I worshipped from afar. You wouldn't have let me get any closer anyway. Then you walked in on me the other night, and I found I still loved you. And when they brought Terry in and I covered his face and they talked to me, even when I sat in the waiting-room in the hospital, and they stitched his face together, even then all I could think was, "I'm glad they didn't do this to my David." Wasn't that foolish of me?'

'No,' said Callan. 'Not foolish.'

'Oh but it was. You see you're not my David and never will be – and they could still do to you what they did to Terry. All they have to do is find you – and with your eyes as they are–'

Callan said, 'They don't want to carve me, Groper. They want to kill me.'

He would have stopped there, but the Groper said, 'This time it really is your turn to talk.'

'All right,' said Callan. 'That's why they wouldn't let you help me. That's why they carved Terry. It wasn't anything personal. They've got nothing against queers. They've got nothing against anybody who doesn't get in their way. But you did get in their way. You were going to give me drops for my eyes. And they want me blind, Groper. It'll be so much easier to kill me if I'm blind.'

'I can't help you. Not now,' the Groper said. 'It took all the nerve I had just to come and see you.'

Callan said gently, 'I'm not asking you. You've done enough.'

'No,' the Groper said. 'I love you. But I'm too afraid. What's his name got it wrong you know. All that stuff about perfect love casteth out fear. On the contrary. It's perfect fear that casts out love. I'm sorry my dear.'

'Don't be,' said Callan. 'If there's any blame, it's mine. I called you.'

'Who are they, David?' the Groper asked.

Again Callan's voice was gentle. 'Better leave it,' he said. 'You know too much already.'

'Can't you – do anything?'

'I can kill them,' said Callan.

The Groper said, 'My poor love.'

He got to his feet, dabbed at the grass and smears of green on his hands and face, then took a small, flat box from his pocket.

'I've never bought you anything,' he said, 'though God knows I've wanted to. The right clothes, the right jewelry – all that. It's a pity but this seems to be the only present I'll ever give you. But don't try to put them in yourself, dear. See if you can find a medical friend with a few more guts than me.'

He dropped the box into Callan's hand.

'It came a day early,' the Groper said. 'I'm glad I at least had the guts to give it to you.'

He was gone as Callan tried to read the label. It was a box of eye-drops.

12

Callan dialled the long number that he could never forget. As always, she answered immediately.

'Yes?'

'Let me speak to Charlie please,' said Callan. For once he got a gasp of surprise from that glacial calm.

'I don't know–' she began.

'Find out,' said Callan. It took a minute, which was half the time he was going to allow before he hung up, then Hunter came on.

'Charlie speaking,' said Hunter. 'How are you, David old chap?'

'You mean you don't know?'

'About your eyes? Of course I knew. You were very evasive, but not quite evasive enough. You should realise by now that you have no secrets from me.'

'So you passed that information on along with all the rest?'

Hunter said, 'I did not.'

'Don't lie to me, Hunter.'

'I never lie to Section Operatives. You know that.'

'I'm not a section operative – you know *that*.'

Hunter said, 'I hear you killed one of them.'

'Yeah,' said Callan. 'A dog-lover.'

'The other two won't be so careless,' said Hunter.

'They can see better than I can,' Callan said. 'And they know where I go for treatment because you told them.'

'If what you say is true it's due to your own carelessness, Callan. I've told them nothing.'

'Goodbye,' said Callan.

'Wait. I want to–'

'You want to trace this call while we're chatting,' Callan said. 'Don't bother. I'm at Piccadilly Tube Station. Tell your friends if you like. I won't be here when they arrive.'

'Callan! Wait,' said Hunter, then winced as the other phone slammed down. Callan really had left the Section. For the first time in his life he'd hung up on Hunter.

Meres put down the ear-piece and waited. When Hunter looked like that it was better to let him start the conversation.

'You look quite bewildered,' Hunter said at last. 'It suits you.' Meres stayed silent. 'Are you bewildered?'

'About his eyes?' said Meres. 'No, sir. It was on his file.'

'Did you pass it on, Toby?'

Meres said carefully, 'You didn't tell me to, sir.'

'No,' said Hunter. 'I didn't, did I?'

'Does Callan say I did?'

'He appears to think that somebody did,' Hunter said. 'What Callan thinks is usually correct.' He thought for a moment. 'You know Toby, showing initiative can be an excellent thing, but only if it succeeds.'

Meres tried to speak, but Hunter cut him short.

'Tell me about Zhilkov,' he said.

'He's very happy up at the manor,' Meres said. 'Eating well. Sleeping well.'

'Drinking?'

'Not a problem,' said Meres. 'He's very – relaxed.'

'And the debriefing?'

Meres said, 'He'd talk all day if we let him. The trouble is he doesn't know all that much.'

'You surprise me,' said Hunter.

'He's got a lot of background stuff,' Meres said. 'Stuff we can use. But it's all minor. You know what I think sir?'

'That they were on to him long before they arrested him,' said Hunter. 'That they switched codes and operatives – and didn't tell him. That the stuff they did tell him wasn't true. That's what you think, Meres. And I think so too.'

Meres said, 'He's not much of a bargain for Callan, is he sir?'

Hunter stared at him, and Meres waited for the explosion. It didn't come.

'You don't lack courage, do you Toby?' Hunter said at last. 'But at least you have right on your side. He isn't much of a bargain. But it's a bargain I must keep.'

'But sir–'

'We got Zhilkov out,' said Hunter. 'The other side know that. It'll be all over Dzerzhinsky Street by now– Gossip is the curse of this business. But this time it's useful gossip. Because if we ever get hold of another Zhilkov he already knows we'll look after him – no matter what it costs. And that, my dear Toby, is vital. We must keep our bargain.'

'And let Callan die?'

'Precisely,' said Hunter. 'But as we both know, his eyesight is at risk. He might well have been of no further use to us anyway.'

Meres realised, not for the first time, that Hunter was the only man he'd ever met of whom he was afraid.

Tube and bus, walk a bit, another bus. Down escalators while the pictures of birds flicked past: birds who wore nothing but tights, or boots, or bras; then sitting looking at other people sitting looking, or reading the paper, then up again past more pictures of birds. Downstairs on the bus because you never could stand the smoke, and nowadays it makes your eyes water. Past shops, past houses, past pubs with people in them –

people who were, for that moment at any rate, happy. Then walk because it's cheaper, through a dusk deepening and intensifying like blindness, except that when this dark comes, the lights come too, and the tellies in the high-rises flicker like constellations. One more bus then, across the river, where the shops and houses are smaller and grimier, and even if people shout more, they're more relaxed. Then fish and chips and tea, two cups, and make the second one last, because the place is warm and the chair's not bad, and until somebody else wants your place at least you've got time to think.

Hunter had said he hadn't lied, but whether he had or not it didn't matter a damn: the killers still knew about his eyes. No. Wait. Whether Hunter had lied or not was important. If he'd lied, they also knew which hospital he had to make for. If Hunter hadn't lied they only knew that Callan, like a berk, had told the Groper on the phone. Aunty Glad's phone. And somebody had bugged it. And if Aunty Glad's why not Lonely's and Aunty Gertie's as well? And if it wasn't Hunter, who the hell else could it be? And how would he be able to get the drops next time he needed them – if they *knew?*

He could feel the panic rising inside him, but panic was something he didn't dare allow to happen. It was panic that had sent him running to Lonely, that had sparked off

176

the whole chain reaction of bugged phones, the carving of Terry, the Groper's grief. If he panicked again he was dead. Fear he could cope with, had to cope with. Throughout the nightmare on the building site he'd been afraid, but he hadn't panicked, and he'd won that round. The only round he had won... He paid his bill then, got up and walked some more, towards the grit and shabbiness of poverty, and the working men's Hilton that would offer him its hospitality for the night, provided he paid in advance.

The place looked like a nick, inside and out. Brick the colour of strong tea, green paint that had been scarred and chipped by experts, the smell of disinfectant only just overpowering the smell of urine. He had the Imperial Suite, him and nineteen others: twenty beds left over from the Crimean War Hospital at Scutari. But at least he had his choice. He was the first to arrive... As beds there was nothing to choose between them; the blankets were equally rough, the mattresses equally flat. The only choice you had was position, and in the end he chose the one nearest the door. There'd be nits barging into him all night going to the lavatory, but at least he'd be able to get out quick in the morning.

Getting ready for sleep was simple. He put his money in his trouser pocket, took off his coat, raincoat, and shoes, spread the coat and raincoat between two blankets, then got into bed, put the shoes under his pillow and took the carrier bag in beside him. This place, he knew, was a rough one: the kind where the patrons stole anything left lying around for the same reason Mallory and Irving climbed Everest: because it was there. He lay back on the cot, adjusting his body to the lumps in the mattress. Sleeping in the nick had been better, sleeping in the jungle in Malaya had been worse. At least by the feel of it so far, there weren't any bugs. He dozed off lightly till the rest of the guests started to arrive.

The first ones weren't drunk. They were probably too broke to achieve that state of bliss, nursing a couple of pints for four hours, avoiding the barmaid's eye. But they barged in anyway, and their whispers, when they thought he was sleeping, were audible at twenty yards. One of them dropped a tool bag on the floor with a sound like cannonfire, then went on whispering. The next lot had obviously had more money, and came in arguing about football. The game they had seen four days ago was fresher in their minds than the work they'd done that afternoon, almost as fresh as the memory of the beer they'd just finished drinking. Callan rolled over in his bed and tried not to listen, and remembered a psychology lecture he'd once had on total recall.

The last lot came in singing. None of your

pop stuff: none of your beat numbers. Not for them. It was a grand, old-fashioned ballad with heart in it, the kind where you can really let yourself go. Galway Bay. All that lovely stuff about going across the sea to Ireland, and moonrise and the sun going down. 'Oh the English came and tried to teach us their ways,' they sobbed, and not a bloody Irishman among them, thought Callan. The Irish were still arguing about football. Then one of the singers turned to literature instead, and started quoting the Three Bears.

'Somebody's sleeping in my bed,' he said.

Oh God, thought Callan. This is all I needed. He opened his eyes to find that he was looking at a large and muscular baritone who had suddenly lost his need for music.

'You're sleeping in my bed,' the man said, and Callan prepared to get out of it. There was no sense in starting a fight; the last thing he wanted was to have the coppers in.

'I always sleep in that bloody bed,' said the man, and Callan sat up and reached for his shoes, whereupon the baritone, recognising a sign of weakness, aimed a blow at him. For a blow from a drunk, it came fast and accurate, and Callan only just ducked his head in time. The baritone was already aiming the next one when Callan threw a shoe into his face, and the blow turned into a shielding gesture to protect his eyes as Callan slid out of bed.

'Look,' said Callan, 'you can have this bed.'

The baritone aimed a kick at him, and Callan lost his temper. His body arched away from the kick, and the baritone staggered, grabbing for balance. Callan's arm came up and the edge of his hand caught the baritone just below the nose. The bed he fell on wasn't Callan's, and its occupant swore loudly, as one of the Irish football fans yelled a warning. Callan swung round to face another singer with a bottle and ducked under its swing, taking a blow from the man's upper arm on the side of his head, a stupid blow that didn't even daze him, but he wanted to sleep for God's sake. This whole ruddy business was ridiculous. He grabbed the lapels of the man's jacket and pulled, twisting his fists into the throat. The man gasped and turned scarlet, and Callan went on twisting and pulling, forcing him to his knees. When the gasping had almost ceased Callan let him go. The man stayed on his knees, making terrible sounds of pain as he tried to breathe. Callan took the bottle from him – it contained stout – and threw it to the Irishman who'd yelled the warning.

'Get yourselves to bed,' he said, 'and don't let's have any more bloody nonsense.'

Someone dragged the baritone away, someone helped the kneeling man to a distant corner, someone handed Callan his shoe. Nobody said a word.

Farce. Callan thought. That's all I bloody

180

needed. Singing drunks and a punch-up with the soloist and his mate. And that makes me cock of the hostel. You've come up in the world, haven't you? Once you were only cock of 'E' Wing in Pentonville Prison. Mind you, you've learned a few more dirty tricks since then. You damn fool, what do you think you're playing at? If you'd gone on the way you started you'd have killed the pair of them, and with the stuff you know, that would have been murder. Back inside for fifteen years at least – for a couple of idiots who didn't even know where to hit...

But in the morning, he found that he was wrong. The man with the bottle had known exactly where to hit. The blow on the side of the head had brought back his double vision. Even a trained K.G.B. man and a couple of killer dogs hadn't achieved that, but this nit had managed it with one blow from his biceps. Carefully, Callan looked about him. Blurred double images told him that every bed was occupied, and it was time to go. He put on his coat, raincoat and shoes, picked up his carrier bag and made for the the door, reeling like a drunk. If the baritone caught him now he could eat him up. But somehow he escaped without a sound, and looked at his watch, decided it was six in the morning, and knew beyond doubting that he had the worst headache of his life, that he had to get to the hospital, and that if he did his killers might be waiting for him.

He walked the streets and risked a quick cup of coffee at a caff and prayed to God a copper wouldn't spot him and decide he was drunk, then bought aspirin from a slot-machine and the headache receded, but the double vision didn't. He had to get to the hospital. At eight thirty the shops started to open, and at nine he found what he wanted – a 'do it yourself' painters' and decorators'. He went inside and bought three feet of white curtain rod, then moved on to a secondhand clothes shop, where he looked around like a pop-eyed idiot and worried the life out of the old girl who ran it, but managed to calm her down sufficiently to buy an overcoat that didn't look too bad and a hat that actually looked good. As he fumbled with the money to pay her she started to look worried again, but he handed it over at last, and held his hand still so that she could put the change in it. When he left he wondered which of them was the more relieved.

He found a tube-station with a lavatory then, and had another bad time putting a coin into the lock, then went inside and abandoned the raincoat, put his razor, tooth-brush and change of underwear into the overcoat pockets, and abandoned the carrier bag, then set the hat on his head, put on the dark glasses and held the curtain rod like a stick. All I need, he thought, is the tin cup and the pencils. Blind Pugh Callan; waiting for the Black Spot, tap-tapping his way up the steps from the Underground, then feeling his way along a street of people, office-workers in a rush who nevertheless found time to avoid bumping into him, even if they bumped into everybody else. He waited for somebody to denounce him as a fake, ask him who the hell he thought he was fooling; but it didn't happen. To the people around him he was blind and therefore vulnerable, so they took care not to knock him over, and that was all, until he reached a corner. Then somebody took him by the arm, and he almost dropped his stick and ran for it, till he looked round, with that questing look of the blind, and saw a teen-age girl he'd never seen before.

'You want to be careful, crossing here,' the girl said. 'Shall I see you over?'

'Thanks,' said Callan. 'Thanks very much.'

He was careful not to move before she did, and to keep on using his stick. When she got him over she said, 'Mind how you go,' and was off at a run, and Callan moved on to the next corner, and waited, grateful to the girl for saving him from the stupidity of a life-time. He'd been looking out for a taxi. How can a blind man spot an empty taxi? His next helper couldn't spot one either, and handed him over to a policeman.

'We don't get many round here,' the copper

said. 'Going far?'

'Saint Martin's Hospital,' Callan said.

'Urgent?'

'Bad enough,' said Callan.

'Let's have a look then,' the copper said. 'There's a rank not far. You might be lucky.'

He led Callan to the rank, where one cab stood empty, then went to the shelter, came back with the driver, and helped Callan in. When they got to the main gate of the hospital, the driver led him up the steps then charged him half-fare, and nothing Callan could say would make him take more.

'Never you mind arguing,' he said. 'You just take care of yourself me old son, and mind how you go.'

Callan walked along the corridor towards the ophthalmology ward and knew that someone was following him. But when he looked behind the corridor was empty. Bastard had taken cover. Too late to do anything about it now... He hid his stick behind a radiator, took off his glasses, and fumbled his way to Nurse Somerset's door. He knocked once, and there was no answer. He knocked again, then opened the door. The room was empty, but the door on the other side opened, and the surgeon came out.

'Mr—?'

'Callan.'

'Oh yes. Excuse me. I was expecting my nurse. Is something wrong?'

'Yes,' said Callan. 'I've got the double vision again.'

'I see,' the surgeon said. 'Come inside and let me look at you.' They went into the surgery, and Callan sat as the surgeon examined him.

'At least it doesn't seem any worse,' he said.

'No better either,' said Callan.

From the outer office he heard the brisk tap tap of heels; the rustle of a coat removed.

'No, I'm afraid not,' the surgeon said. 'You still need surgery. Put your head back please.'

The drops came then, soothing, healing.

'How did it happen?' the surgeon said.

'Pardon?'

'Mr Callan you're not a fool. Nor am I. What did you do to cause this?'

Callan said, 'Somebody bumped into me. I banged my head.'

'Where?' Callan showed him. 'Outside? In the street?'

'That's right,' said Callan.

'I don't think you should go out too often on your own,' the surgeon said.

'*You and me both mate.*'

'–Because I don't think your eyes will stand many more bumps. Or indeed, any more bumps. You must take care of yourself, you know.'

'I try to.'

185

Believe me I try to.

The sea-spray brightness in front of his eyes intensified, and Callan knew it was about to clear. When it did the door opened, and the first thing he saw was Nurse Somerset.

'I'm sorry sir,' she said. 'My bus was late.'

'That's all right,' the surgeon said. 'It's time I had a little chat with Mr. Callan anyway. Is anyone else here?'

'Mrs. Charlton.'

'Get her ready will you?' Nurse Somerset left. 'How is it now?' the surgeon asked.

'Clearing,' said Callan. 'I've been thinking – if it happened again, wouldn't it be better if you gave me the prescription for those drops and I went to a doctor somewhere nearer?'

'If it happens again I want to see you.'

'Well of course,' said Callan. 'But if it was an emergency–'

'If it was an emergency,' the surgeon said, 'he could phone me – and I could decide what would be the best thing to do.'

'But–'

'I really am thinking of you,' the surgeon said. 'I know quite a bit about your eyes now, Mr. Callan. Other doctors may not.'

'I just thought I'd mention it,' said Callan.

'I'm very glad you did. Would you mind waiting outside please?'

He went through the nurse's room, where Nurse Somerset was unwinding a bandage

186

from a fat woman's right eye, and sat on a bench in the corridor. Five minutes later she came out to him.

'I was afraid you might have gone,' she said.

'Gone?' said Callan. 'I love it here.'

'You've had more drops,' she said, her voice accusing.

'I go out alone and get bumped into,' Callan said. 'The trouble is I've got no-one to go out with me. Not unless you'd like to.'

'I'd like to very much,' she said; his look of astonishment was genuine.

'You would?' he said.

'Anything to see you don't get bumped into.'

They made a date for that night. Unless I'm still being followed, Callan thought.

13

That day Lonely was to be at the pub near the market, and Callan phoned him at lunchtime, as they'd arranged. It was the potman who answered, and told him Lonely wasn't there. He got the same answer each time he called. After that he tried the house where he lived, but he wasn't there either. Callan sweated, and remembered what had happened to Terry. If they got hold of Lonely– He had to find him, see him, make sure the little man was all right. Aunty Glad's. That was out – seeing her brought too many problems – and Aunty Gertie detested him. But at least she looked out for Lonely. Aunty Gertie it would have to be.

She closed up her coffee-stall at tea time, when the market closed, but she and Lonely usually stayed on and ate there. If he didn't show up till the place was closed, there was at least a chance that the killers wouldn't be watching for him... He thought of phoning the coffee-stall, and decided against it. That phone could be bugged too, like Aunty Glad's. He didn't want them there waiting for him. He took himself to the pictures, and watched more cowboys till it was time to go, then sat on a bus and carried his piece of curtain rod like a good little commuter going home to improve his property. When he changed buses he put on the dark glasses and tapped with the stick, and people helped him on. Callan, master of disguise, he thought. At least it worked: if whoever had followed him hadn't passed it on. The conductor even helped him off and aimed him at the market.

The women had gone. Mostly it was stall-holders now, counting the take, easing out the time till the pubs opened and they could lubricate throats hoarse with shouting. Callan tapped his way among them, and they moved aside not looking, intent only on copper and silver and grubby handfuls of notes. His stick rooted among cabbage leaves, turnip tops, the battered remnants of flowers, and he reached the coffee-stall at last, and felt his way to the back door. Two voices: Aunty Gertie's and Lonely's, and no sign of anyone but the market men, still counting money. Callan knocked at the door.

'We're closed,' Aunty Gertie said. Callan kept on knocking, till the door was flung wide and Aunty Gertie faced him in the awful majesty of her wrath.

'What's the matter with you?' she said. 'Are you bloody deaf or something?' Then her voice checked, and she said gently, 'I'm sorry dear. But we really are closed. I can manage you a cup of tea if you like.'

189

Behind her Lonely said, 'It's Mr. Callan.'

That made her madder than ever, and Callan had to push her back inside and shut the door before she roused the whole market.

'Listen a minute,' he kept saying. 'Just listen,' and for a moment it seemed that she might, till Lonely said, 'Clever that blind dodge, Mr. Callan. I nearly didn't recognise you meself' – and that started her off again.

At last Callan said, 'Did you hear about the Groper's friend?' and found he had silence. Aunty Gertie had heard.

'They carved him,' she said at last. 'I never heard of anybody round here being carved, not for years and years.'

'You never heard of *anybody* being carved the way they carved him,' said Callan.

'Your fault was it?' she asked.

'No,' said Callan. 'It wasn't me that did it.'

'It was because of you though, wasn't it?'

'It was,' said Callan.

'Christ,' Aunty Gertie said. 'You really are bad news,' then added surprisingly, 'Help yourself to a cup of tea. And Lonely – make your mate a sandwich.'

'Thanks,' said Callan.

'Don't thank me,' said Aunty Gertie. 'It's just that I can't stand watching people not eating when I'm eating meself.' She bit at a salt beef sandwich as if it were an enemy, and Lonely built up a vast doorstep of

190

tinned salmon and tomato.

'I suppose you come here to make us bad news an' all,' said Aunty Gertie.

'I came to find out why he wasn't at the pub when I phoned him.'

'He was,' Aunty Gertie said. 'I wouldn't let him answer.'

'You wouldn't let him take a phone call?'

'Not from you,' Aunty Gertie said.

There was no point in asking how she'd got it out of Lonely that he was phoning him. Anyone with Aunty Gertie's muscles and staying power could get anything out of Lonely.

'I had to talk to him,' Callan said. 'That's why I came here. You may not believe this love – but I'm risking my neck coming here.'

'I believe you,' Aunty Gertie said. 'You're also risking his neck – and mine.'

'Not yours,' said Callan. 'Not unless you help me – and there isn't much chance of that happening.'

'None at all,' Aunty Gertie said.

'But Lonely already has,' said Callan. 'So has the Groper.'

She looked at him, her rage controlled now, and then her glance moved to Lonely. Her ugly duckling, who needed more care than all the cygnets. 'You better tell it,' she said.

Callan turned to Lonely.

'I want you to watch it,' he said. 'Night and

day I want you to watch it. Don't go out alone, don't go away from crowds, don't answer the door at night to anyone – not even if you think it's me. And don't do any jobs.'

'No thieving?'

'Do you really want to be out on your own at night – after what happened to Terry?'

The smell came then.

'Now see what you've done,' Aunty Gertie said, then rummaged in her bag and took out money, counting carefully.

'Nip round to the off-licence and get a half bottle of whisky,' she said. 'And mind, there's seven pence change and I want it.'

'Whisky gives me heartburn,' said Lonely.

'Nobody said you got to drink it,' said Aunty Gertie, then relented, and handed over more money. 'Get yourself some beer.'

Lonely left before she could change her mind.

'And do like your mate says,' she shouted after him. 'Stay in the crowd.'

Callan said, 'I hadn't realised you loved him so much.'

'I lost both me own,' she said. 'Motor-bike accident – Kingston by-pass. Lonely's all I've got.' The rage had gone now. All she could do was plead. 'Stay away from him, mister.'

'I want to,' said Callan, 'but it's just possible he may need me.'

'Fighting,' she said. 'You'd be good at that.' Callan said nothing. 'He tells me you got him out of trouble once. He reckons he owes you.'

'Not any more,' said Callan.

'That's what I tell him,' she said, 'but he won't listen.'

There was anger again in the thought that Lonely wouldn't listen to his Aunty Gertie, but there was pride too.

'That all you came for – just to warn him?'

'I had to know he was all right,' said Callan.

'You really risked your neck for my nephew?'

'I let him risk his for me.'

'You really are a mate,' Aunty Gertie said. 'But I still don't want him hurt.'

'Keep him away from your sister Glad,' said Callan.

'Glad's no sister of mine. She's on Lonely's father's side. Stuck-up tart. What's she been up to then?'

'Had her phone bugged,' Callan said. 'She let me use it. That's how they got on to the Groper's friend.'

'Silly cow,' said Aunty Gertie. 'She ought to have more sense.'

Callan said, 'I thought she had.'

'Oh she's got all her marbles that one. And a few more.'

'Fond of Lonely isn't she?' Callan asked.

'When she remembers. Don't worry. I'll see Lonely doesn't go near. Anything else?'

193

'That phone idea of mine – it makes sense. Honestly it does,' said Callan. 'At least he can let me know if he needs help.'

'Why can't he phone you direct?'

'Because I'm on the move,' said Callan.

Her eyes took in his rumpled suit, unshaven face.

'Sleeping rough, are you?'

'Rough enough.'

'I could let you have a few quid. Just a loan like.'

'No thanks,' said Callan. She didn't renew the offer. 'But you could let me shave,' he said.

'Help yourself.'

When Lonely came back with the whisky and beer, Callan was shaving in front of a scrap of mirror, and Aunty Gertie was sitting comfortably, hands folded in her lap, listening to the soft rasp of the razor.

'I do like to watch a man shaving,' she said, and smiled. 'Blimey – it takes me back a year or two.' Lonely almost dropped the bottle. 'Mind what you're doing with that whisky. Here give it to me you clumsy great nit.'

She rummaged in a cupboard, and produced a couple of crystal tumblers, and a silver tankard with a crest so worn as to be indecipherable.

'Pour your own,' she said to Lonely, and passed him the tankard. 'Me and your mate's on the Scotch.'

194

She smiled at his bewilderment.

'He's going to phone you every day like you agreed,' she said.

'You mean you don't mind?' said Lonely.

'Mind? Of course I mind. Only I don't have any choice. No more do you.' She looked at Callan, washing the remains of shaving-soap from his face.

'At least he means well,' she said. 'And a fat lot of bloody good that is.'

Lonely grinned.

'I told you Mr. Callan was a real mate.'

'Let's hope he stays one when he gets out of his bit of trouble,' Aunty Gertie said, and poured out Scotch; then, as Lonely started to argue: 'Don't back answer your Auntie, Lonely. Drink your beer and I'll walk you home.'

'No hurry,' said Lonely. 'I don't have to get an early kip now, seeing I'm not going to be doing no jobs.'

'We'll see about that,' Aunty Gertie said. 'All we agreed was no jobs for the time being. You haven't started drawing your bloody pension.'

He'd arranged to meet her at a pub by the river, an old pub that looked across at Wren's cathedral, and was packed with tourists. He knew her well enough to get there ahead of time, and wait near the door so that she didn't have to undergo the usual agony of shyness pushing her way through, trying to find him. She saw him waiting, and smiled.

'You picked a fine place to avoid people bumping into you,' she said.

Callan turned sideways, and made just enough room for her to stand beside him.

'You're supposed to do that,' he said. 'What would you like? Shandy?'

'Rum,' she said. 'I'm feeling homesick.'

They drank and talked, and drank again. The talk was light and teasing: it couldn't be anything else when your nearest neighbour was inches away, but it was good talk, and the laughter came easily from her, but the tension, Callan knew, was still there, and it seemed to him in greater strength than before.

'I like this place,' she said.

'Better than the Greyhound?'

'I *really* like it,' she said. 'But we can't talk here.'

'Another rum?'

'Maybe later. What I'd really like to do now is go somewhere more quiet.'

'Take a walk?'

'If you can get out of here without being bumped into,' she said.

Somehow he managed it, and they walked along the riverside, stopped and stared at the cathedral, marvelled and walked on to where Callan showed her a narrow, slender house, dainty as a doll's house, its seventeenth

196

century prettiness raddled by decay.

'Oh what a shame,' she said. 'It's lovely. Who lived here?'

'Sir Christopher Wren,' he said. 'He could wake up every morning, look out of the window and see how his cathedral was doing.'

She looked from the house's miniature elegance to the great church's massive solemnity. 'At home you never realise,' she said. 'This is all just pictures in books.' She turned and faced him, and her smile was enchanting, but beneath it the tensions still plagued her. 'Would you like to eat?' she said.

'Anything you say,' said Callan. At this rate he'd end up kipping in the park.

'I know just the place,' she said.

They took a bus back across the river, then walked through a tangled maze of streets past a factory going full blast. The noise was deafening.

'Good God,' said Callan.

'They make metal boxes,' she said.

Behind them there sounded an enormous crash.

'And drop them,' Callan said.

They walked on past a row of derelict houses, then turned a corner to a street of gaunt Victorian villas cut up into flats, and the row receded; the sound of the river became audible once more. She led him to one of the houses and walked down the steps to the area. Callan followed.

197

'Funny place for a restaurant,' he said.

'I live here,' she said. 'You know I live here. I want you to come inside.'

She unlocked the door and he followed her in. Tiny bathroom, tiny kitchen, and one big room that was bedroom, drawing-room, dining-room combined, a place where servants had once laboured, where the windows scarcely revealed the light of day. But it wasn't a room to be looked at in daylight. The curtains were already drawn as she switched on the light. Callan looked around him. The room echoed her sickness for home.

The walls were white and blue, like white stone beside a warm sea, the rug on the floor was yellow as sunshine, the pictures were all travel posters of Barbados; white beaches, black faces, palms silhouetted against the ocean. A bookcase split the room in two, and the dust-jackets added their light and colour to the rest. Callan moved across to it. One shelf held wood-carvings instead of books; the head of a young negress, a pair of dancers, an old man with a donkey. Behind him Nurse Somerset moved about, switching on radiators and fires. Callan had never seen so many in one room.

'You'd better take your coat off,' she said. 'It gets very warm in here.'

'I'm not surprised,' said Callan.

'I hope you don't mind,' she said. 'But until

198

just recently I was never cold in my life.'

'I don't mind,' he said.

She took his coat and her own, and hung them up in the hallway. The dress she wore was white, and round her neck was a string of amber beads.

'You look very beautiful,' he said.

'Thank you.'

They were words she wanted to hear, and she was well aware of their truth, so why the tension?

'These wood carvings are nice,' said Callan.

'They were done by a man who used to be my fiancé,' she said. 'Everybody says he was very talented.'

'Used to be your fiancé?'

'He died,' she said.

'I'm sorry,' said Callan, then: 'I like the way you've done this room.'

She smiled. 'I'm glad you like it. Pour the drinks please.'

He moved to a trolley with bottles on it.

'Please pour big ones,' she said. 'With lots of ice. Then we can pretend we've flown home for dinner.'

She went to the kitchen while he poured, and the heat in the room mounted, the smell of spices came through the open door. When she came back he was mopping his face with his handkerchief.

'I think you should take your jacket off too,' she said. 'Where I used to live – white shirt and tie is formal evening wear.'

He did as she suggested and brought her drink to her. She sipped at once.

'Delicious,' she said. 'Thank you.' Then, in a rush: 'I want to tell you something.'

'Go ahead,' said Callan.

'Apart from me you're the only person who's ever been in here,' she said. 'Isn't that ridiculous?'

'No,' said Callan. 'It's sad.'

'Oh but you're wrong,' she said. 'I *like* being on my own.'

'I know,' said Callan. 'All that reading. All the politics and sociology and economics. All that important boredom.'

'I should have warned you that sometimes I'm a very pompous person,' she said. 'Lonely people often are. Are you ever pompous?'

'Who told you I was lonely?'

'You did,' she said. 'You said you had nobody to go out with. And anyway I know enough about it by now to recognise the signs. Do you mind if we talk about you?'

'Not so far,' he said.

'I think you're lonely by choice – like me. We could have friends if we wanted. But I don't have any. Not one. Do you have friends?'

'I've got a mate,' said Callan.

'Is there a difference?'

'I think there is,' he said. 'It's a bit subtle

200

to put into words, but it's there.'

'One friend between us. And otherwise –
what? Bus conductors, shop assistants,
people in pubs, the people we work with.'

'I don't have any work,' said Callan. 'Not
just at the moment.'

'Oh my God,' she said. 'And I let you pay
for all those drinks.'

'You couldn't have stopped me,' said
Callan. 'I'm bigger than you are.'

A pan in the kitchen hissed and spattered,
and she yelled, 'Bully' as she ran to the
kitchen, then called out again for him to
pour more drinks. He took them to her as
she anxiously tested and stirred.

'I thought I'd burnt it,' she said. 'But I
didn't.'

'What is it?' Callan asked. 'It smells marvellous.'

'Pepper-pot,' she said. 'It's really a Trinidad
dish but my mother loved it. We ate it a lot.
Lucky I always liked to cook.'

'What's in it?'

'Chicken and pigs' trotter and onions and
chillies and spices and our very own magic
ingredient called cassareep. That's awfully
difficult to come by over here.'

Callan inhaled the aroma of the food.

'By the smell of that – we're in the West
Indies,' he said.

'Oh David – if only we were.'

'Does that mean I can use your first

201

name?' Callan asked.

'Before I said I wasn't sure I wanted you to. I'm sure now,' she said. 'Please call me Amanda– And put some knives and forks on the table.'

They sat down then to the best meal Callan had eaten in days, and finished it off with a pineapple that he said was vast, and she dismissed as one of those midget things they grow in Jamaica. Then there was coffee, with rum in it, and this time she insisted that he had rum in his coffee too. She brought it to him on the divan, that now did duty as a sofa.

'You're trying to get us drunk,' he said.

'No,' she said. 'Not drunk. Just warm. And happy. Like we used to be in Barbados.' She drank her coffee again, then turned to face him.

'I don't want to talk any more,' she said.

'Don't do anything you don't want to do,' said Callan and kissed her. Her lips were cool and moist and responsive, her body firm yet infinitely yielding, and yet he drew away from her, waited until her eyes opened and looked into his.

'I mean it,' he said.

'I won't,' said Amanda. 'I promise you I won't,' and moved back into his arms.

The warmth of their clothes was too much to be borne, and they struggled free of them and went back to each other at once, seeking a closeness that would reduce the world to themselves, only themselves, and the aching joy each could give the other. At first she reached out for him with a fierce impatience, but he made her hold back, till the time was perfect and their bodies blended, rhythmic and easy, and the world was themselves and the joy each gave the other.

They looked at each other at last in happiness and amazement at what they had made together.

'I feel smug,' she said.

'Smug?'

'I never thought I–' she hesitated. 'All right. I withdraw smug. I feel happy.'

He kissed her.

'Then you know how I feel,' he said.

She left him then, and presently came back with more coffee. He took his carefully, wary of his nakedness, and she laughed.

'It's a little late for that,' she said, and looked at his body. She hadn't covered hers. It was perfect, as he had known it would be. Suddenly she reached out to take his shoulder, turned him sideways, and looked at his back.

'You've got an awful lot of scars,' she said. 'Here, and here, and here.'

She touched the places where the knife wound, the two bullet wounds, had healed at last into pale lines on his skin.

'I told you,' he said. 'I used to be a soldier.'

But none of these came from Malaya. Hunter supplied them all.

'You really killed people?'

'And people tried to kill me.'

'I'm sorry it had to be like that.'

'It was a long time ago,' said Callan.

She gulped her coffee, then came back to his arms. She was as relaxed as a cat, but there was still the cat-like awareness about her, too.

'Now's when I want to talk,' she said.

'Talk then.'

'About what you do.'

'You know what I do. Nothing. I'm un-employed.'

'On your form you said you were a book-keeper.'

'So?'

'I don't think you are.'

He'd been ready for it. His hands on her body stayed easy and relaxed. 'What do you think I am?'

'I don't know,' she said. 'But you're in danger. I'm sure you are.'

'Do I look afraid?'

'You look – ready,' she said. 'It's hard to explain.' Her finger traced the bullet scar across his chest; they'd had to dig deep for that one. 'All this – it's what I watch in the cinema. But with you – you do it. You really do it.'

'You think I'm a crook?'

'I wouldn't mind,' she said. 'Honestly I wouldn't... Isn't that why you move around all the time?'

'Yeah,' said Callan. 'That's why.'

Her body stayed evenly pressed against his, the finger that traced his scar moved steadily along it.

'Shouldn't you ask if I'm a murderer?' he said.

'I don't want to know.' Her finger moved to the knife wound on his back.

'I can help you,' she said.

'Can you?'

'I can let you stay here. You'd like to stay here – the food's good. Isn't the food good?'

'Almost as good as the service,' said Callan. 'But I can't.'

'Why not?'

'You might get hurt.'

'I'll risk that.'

'Listen to me,' he said. 'The people after me are good at hurting people. It's their job.' She shuddered then. 'But there's one thing you can do.'

'Yes?'

'I got a box of eyedrops. Let me leave them here. You could put them in for me – if I couldn't get to the hospital.'

'That's all?'

'It might be enough – if those fellers I told you about got to hear of it.'

Her finger moved to the scar on his thigh.

She said, 'I think we've talked enough.'

This time their love was slow and rhythmic from the start, moving inevitably from tenderness to strength, like a flower unfolding, till she cried out loud to the pleasure she had made, the movement of her body eased and stilled.

'I never yelled like that before,' she said. 'You know Whitey – you've made a poor coloured girl very happy.'

'I aim to please,' said Callan.

'Whitey you done hit the bullseye, and if that's a Freudian slip I'm proud of it. Come and take a shower.'

They stood together in the tiny bathroom soaping, sponging each other, the trickling water's coolness one more pleasure in a night of pleasure. At last she switched off the shower, took towels and began to dry his body. When he reached for her, she moved away.

'Your turn's next,' she said. When he'd dried her she perfumed her body and then said, 'Let me – please.'

'What now?' said Callan.

'Let me put some on you. I want us to smell the same.'

When she'd done she said, 'You didn't laugh at me.'

'Why should I?'

'Oh Whitey, Whitey,' she said. 'You're so perfect it frightens me... Let's have some more coffee.'

When it came there was rum in it.

'You must have a head like old teak,' said Callan.

'Well anyway, you got the colour right,' she said. He slapped her and she yelled. 'White Fascist pig,' she said.

Carefully Callan said, 'I thought pigs were coppers.'

'Pigs are people who beat up poor coloured girls,' she said.

'This pig's in clover,' said Callan.

'You say the nicest things.' She laughed, and the rum was in her laughter.

'I think it's time you went to bed,' said Callan, and the laughter went on.

'The very nicest things,' she said. He reached for his clothes.

'Oh no,' she said. 'I'm not going to bed if you're not.'

'I have to go,' said Callan.

'No you don't. You can stay here with me tonight. You'll be safe with me.'

'All right,' said Callan. 'Thanks.'

'Such an eloquent lover.'

She dragged him to his feet then, pulled the slip-cover from the divan, and lay on it. Callan switched off the fires and the lights and lay down beside her.

'No you don't,' she said. 'You and I don't sleep like that.' Her hands reached out, caressing.

'Say my name,' she said.

'Amanda.'

'You know what it means?'

'You tell me.'

'It's from the Latin,' she said. 'It means "fit to be loved".'

'It couldn't mean anything else,' said Callan.

14

When she woke, he was gone. Her head ached in the first stages of hangover, but the weariness of her body was a remembered pleasure. What she had done she had done willingly, and her body felt it, even though her mind still nagged at the complications that Callan had brought into her life... He must have moved very quietly to escape from her arms without her knowing. Had he kissed her, she wondered, before he left? There was no note, nor had she expected one. When he needed her again, he would be back. Of that she was sure, and the thought frightened her. She had learned the violence in the man, even at his most tender...

Patiently Callan watched the house. She had earned that at least, and perhaps he had too. The solace of her body had been something desperately needed; generously given, even when her mind still nagged at the kind of man he had been, and still was. All that talk of the killing he had done in Malaya: the terrible need to know why he had done it, what it was like to kill. Question after question. And yet only once had her body been other than soft and open to him: that time

209

when he'd told her that he'd volunteered for the Commandos. Her whole body had clenched then, a swift, reflexive act of denial, until, so it seemed, her mind took over, and she willed herself back to acquiescence, to acceptance of the need they both shared. The word love had never passed between them. They'd never make it as romantics, he thought. They were both too damned honest...When the time came to go he found that he was yawning. Find a caff for breakfast, he thought, and then if the sun shone, take a kip in the park. Phone her first maybe. She was the most remarkable woman he'd ever met. And the most beautiful by far.

'I didn't think you'd leave me like that,' she said.

Callan said, 'Neither did I.'

'Why then–'

'I don't want you hurt because of me.'

She said quickly, 'I told you I didn't care.'

'Maybe you don't,' said Callan. 'But I do.'

'How are your eyes?' she asked.

'Never better. My nurse gives me the right treatment. How's your head?'

'Terrible,' she said.

'Next time don't drink so much.'

'What makes you so sure there'll be a next time?'

'No man in his right mind would ever take you for granted,' he said. 'Please can there be a next time?'

'Damn you,' she said. 'Why don't you fight fair?'

'I don't want to fight at all,' he said.

Then the doctor came in, and the first of the endless stream of patients, each one demanding all her tact and skill even though her head still ached, and her body remembered.

His sleep in the park was wary and fitful, and when he dreamed it was of the jungle in Malaya, and that wasn't surprising. The surprise was in the Chinese he killed. When he turned them over, they had the faces of Karski, Lebichev, Kliegmann: the ones he'd killed for Hunter; the reasons why he himself was now going to die. The sun went behind clouds and he got up quickly, swerving to avoid a kid who rode a tricycle as if it were a device for maiming adults. Better to keep moving when he started having thoughts like that. Anyway it was time to call Lonely. He found a phone booth, and the little man answered at once. He sounded worried.

'There's a geezer been following me,' he said.

'Is he on to you now?'

'No,' said Lonely. 'I ditched him, early on.'

'You're sure?'

'Mr Callan – when you're built like me you got to be sure.'

'All right,' said Callan. 'Mind how you go.

211

Keep away from the market today.'

'It's Thursday,' said Lonely. 'The market's closed Thursdays.'

'Just as well,' said Callan. They won't know where to look for you. And Lonely – better not sleep at your place tonight.'

'Where am I supposed to go then?'

'Your Aunty Gertie's,' Callan said. 'Remember that. Your Aunty Gertie's. *Not* your Aunty Glad's.'

'She wouldn't have me,' Lonely said. 'But don't you worry about me, Mr. Callan. I'll be all right. Me Aunty Gertie's staying at my place.'

'No,' said Callan. 'That's out. You stay with her.'

Lonely started to argue, but there wasn't time to be nice, even to a mate.

'Where is she now?' he asked.

'Giving my place a clean-up,' Lonely said bitterly. 'You should have heard her – the way she went on. Like I was dirty. You know I'm not dirty, Mr. Callan. What I got's just a bit of bad luck as you might say.'

'Listen,' said Callan. 'You get her out of there. Go straight there now and get her out. And once you've got her home – and you're sure you're not followed – you ring me here. How long will it take you?'

'An hour,' said Lonely. 'If she goes quiet. Otherwise it'll be an hour and a half.'

'Ring me in an hour and a half then,' said

212

Callan. 'I'll be here.' He read out the phone number.

'Do me best,' said Lonely, and hung up.

First Terry, thought Callan, and now Lonely. The vulnerable ones: the ones who they can hurt so I'll get mad and go charging to the rescue so they can hurt me: the only friends, the only help I've got. The innocent ones. But not in their book. In their book anyone who helps Callan is guilty. And where does that leave Amanda? He thought of phoning her, but there was no point. Not until he'd heard from Lonely. He went back to the park, and waited for time to pass.

Lonely moved with the quick, nervous scuttle he always used when he was frightened, scurrying along the crowded pavements at a speed that made it look easy – unless somebody tried to follow him. Then they found how difficult it was – but Lonely could have scurried through the massed bands of the Brigade of Guards, trombones and all. Not that anybody was trying to follow him this time. He was sure of that. Even when he was as terrified as he was now, Lonely always knew when he was followed. The terror inside him acted like radar, and it had never let him down; not once. All the same he took extra precautions as he drew near his own street. Made sense, that did. Anybody who wanted to pick him up, they'd be bound to hang around his gaff. It stood to reason. And Mr. Callan had said they knew where his gaff was – and Mr. Callan would know.

He reached his own street corner, still secure, then stopped and looked about him. Nobody there that shouldn't be there, so far as he could see. Milk float going down the road same time as always, two blokes with a van reclaiming a telly and a woman yelling at them – normal that was, in this street. Bunch of kids in a shop doorway eating chips. Should have been at school, only they preferred to stay away and go thieving, as he himself had done. Start young, he thought. It's the only way. Otherwise you might wind up in a steady job instead of – what mate? Instead of running like a loony and hoping you won't get hurt, he thought. Even steady work can't be as bad as that.

He looked up at the windows of his gaff. Glittering, they were. The cleanest windows in the street. And the rest of it'll be the same, he thought. Floors swept, tables scrubbed, clean sheets on the bed, and Aunty Gertie would be in the middle of it all, going like a steam-engine. She's like a mum to me, Lonely thought, and I know it and I'm grateful. But why does she always have to get so bloody violent about it? Then as he watched, the shining windows shattered, the flames leaped out of them even before the sharp crack of the explosion, and when it came glass and slates rained down on the milkman, the two blokes with the telly, the women who now had reason for screaming, the kids who preferred thieving to vulgar fractions. But they didn't hit Lonely. He was too far away.

He ran then, more terrified than ever, but he ran towards his gaff and Aunty Gertie up there in it, straight into a house that was pouring out women into staircases and passages, a lot of them with kids and all of them yelling. He fought his way through them, scrambling up floor by floor, and they let him pass unquestioned. Some of them didn't even see him... At the stairhead below his there was this geezer who worked nightshift sitting there in his pyjamas holding on to the phone and dialling 999, too bloody dazed to see it was blown off the wall. Above that the stairs gave out halfway, the banister rail dangled, blown loose from its supports in the wall. Lonely wedged it under the stairs and went up it like a rope. Getting into his room was no problem. The door was in pieces.

Inside, everything that could burn seemed to be burning; bed, table, chairs. The curtains had disappeared; the paint on the walls was blistering. He looked round, the skin on his face wincing at the heat, choking as the smoke reached at him – and at first he couldn't see Aunty Gertie, and it was wonderful. And then he did see her, and it was the most terrible thing that had ever happened to him. A cupboard lay on her, almost obscuring her body. When he looked closer, he could see her face, half covered by a pillow. But it didn't cover the angle at which her neck lay. There could be no doubt about it. Aunty Gertie was dead.

He slid down the banister rail then, and made his way down. The geezer who worked nightshift had given up trying to telephone and left, the yelling women and kids were doing their yelling in the street. Lonely turned down a passage that led to the back of the house, and came to a glass-panelled door. It was locked, from outside. Without hesitation he took off his cap, wrapped it round his fist, smashed in one of the glass panels, and turned the key in the outside lock. For the first time in his life he had no fear of the landlord's wrath. He crossed the grubby yard and opened the back door. The lane behind the house was empty, and there were no prizes for guessing why. All the action would be in the street. No sense in hanging about the lane when there was a bloody big fire to look at right out in front. Lonely walked to the corner of the lane, then turned away from the house. In the distance, louder as he walked, he could hear the first sirens sound...

An hour and a half passed, and Callan didn't hear from Lonely. Two hours, and still no word. Three hours. He was haunting that bloody phone-box. If a rozzer came past he'd be in dead trouble... But the only ones he saw were in a Panda car, and they had better things to do with their time than chat up a man who was waiting by a phone... Callan watched and worried and waited. If something had happened to Lonely, if *they'd* got at him, then it wouldn't take them long to find out where Callan said he'd take a phone call. On the other hand there was a chance that Lonely had managed to shake loose and for some reason couldn't get to a phone. Maybe he'd even lost the number. To Lonely almost anything was possible. But if Lonely had shaken loose one thing was certain. He'd need Callan. And that meant waiting: there was nothing else for it...

Lonely kept on walking, his stride brisk and purposive; nothing like his usual scuttling run; covering the ground in a straight line-ahead, unaware of the people who passed him, the traffic that roared by; unaware even of where he was, as mile followed mile, and he stopped at red lights, waited for them to change, then kept on going – where didn't matter. Just away. From Aunty Gertie lying there with her neck twisted, from the flames that moved in round her, from the men who'd done it to her, and had tried to do it to him. Away from it; that was all he wanted. Quiet, and a bit of peace. That wasn't too much to ask. And every step he took seemed to make it more possible. Nobody knew him in this place he'd got to, and nobody wanted to know him. And that suited Lonely just fine. He walked past bus stops and tube stations and didn't hesitate. Taking a ride meant making decisions, and Lonely was past all that. The ones who'd done it had already made the decision for him. What he had to do was go away just anywhere, and he was doing it. On his feet.

In fact it was his feet that first warned him he'd walked far enough. They began to hurt him, and at first it didn't matter, then it got worse and mattered a great deal. No matter what, he had to find a place to sit down and rest and think some more about this business of getting away. He found a caff and got in the queue at the counter and took a tray – all he wanted was a cup of tea but some places they wouldn't serve you if you didn't take a tray – and the girl who served him never once looked at him, never stopped talking to her mate that was handing out the cakes and sandwiches about the smashing feller she'd met the night before and the smashing time they'd had. My aunty's dead, he thought. Listen you great stupid cow. It's important. *My aunty's dead.* But she didn't even look at him.

He took his cup to a table and sat, and that was good. His feet felt better at once. It would have been nice to take his shoes off, but he didn't dare risk it: he might never get them on again. So he just sat and rested his feet and tried not to think about Aunty Gertie and the things that had been done to that part of her face the pillow had failed to cover. But he couldn't try hard enough; he couldn't *help* seeing her, until the tears came, and he cried in silence, and searched his pockets for a handkerchief– Not that anybody noticed him, let alone was bothered. Not even the geezer sitting across the table from him, nose buried in a bloody book. Lonely waited, the tears ceased, and he dried his eyes again, and hoped he hadn't dirtied his face with his crying. Not that anybody would be bothered about that, either. Not like his aunty would have. Bawled at him for getting his face dirty, then gone looking for the geezer who'd made him cry. She'd been doing that for him ever since he was four years old. But not this time. This time the geezers had been too big for her.

It was a long while before he could think of anything except him and his aunty; him always behind her, and her always arguing: with truant officers, magistrates, police. Then other times: visiting him in the nick, taking him round the pub when he came out. The nick wasn't such a bad place. Not really. Come to that it was the only place he had to look forward to, now he'd lost his aunty and his gaff. Do a bit of bird and he'd be nicely out of the way – suddenly he remembered Callan. Until that moment there had been no room in his mind for anything except his grief and loss, but now there was Callan, too. Bloody Callan and his bleeding troubles, and all they'd done was get his aunty killed. You go and stuff yourself, Callan, thought Lonely. You and me's finished mate.

But it wouldn't do, and he knew it wouldn't do. Aunty Gertie was dead, and he needed somebody, didn't he? And he'd promised her faithfully he wouldn't go near his Aunty Glad. And something ought to be done about what those geezers had done to her, and Lonely knew *he* wasn't going to do it. He wouldn't know where to start looking. And even if he did he wouldn't. He was too scared. But Callan now – he was different. He'd seen him. That time in the nick. And he hadn't needed a gun then. Maybe he could manage without one this time. At any rate he'd have to try. He owed Aunty Gertie that much. Lonely got up and went to the toilet to wash the tear-stains from his face, then set out to find a telephone...

There was still no sign of Lonely, and Callan knew that it was time to go. Then a woman ran past him, hurrying for a bus, and her newspaper fell off the top of her shopping bag. He picked it up and was going to shout after her, but the bus had gone, and anyway, he'd seen the headline. 'Mystery Blast Rocks

London House.' 'Police Say Bomb May Have Caused Fatality.' He read on, eyes flicking down the page. 'Sudden explosion ... confined to one room on upper floor... Believed one body so far recovered...' And that's it, he thought. Poor little bastard. You should go and live on a desert island mate. Robinson Crusoe Callan. Every time you get next to another human being you destroy them. He screwed the paper up in his hands, let it fall. That was it... Now he *was* on a bloody desert island, and his only Man Friday was dead. Then the phone rang. He went into the booth and picked it up.

'Yes?' he said.

'Is that you, Mr. Callan?'

Callan let out his breath in a long sigh.

'Yes,' he said. 'It's me.'

'I got to see you,' Lonely said.

'All right.'

'Things have been happening,' said Lonely. 'I think you should know about them.'

'Where are you?' said Callan.

'I don't know... I've been walking, you see. Walking and walking. Then me feet gave out. And then I thought – I got to see you.'

'I've just seen the paper,' said Callan.

'I haven't had time to read no paper,' Lonely said. 'Things has been happening. Me Aunty Gertie's dead.'

'That's what I saw in the paper,' said Callan. 'I'm sorry.'

'Ah,' said Lonely. 'And so you should be. Where can we talk?'

'You in a phone booth?' Callan said.

'That's right.'

'Read me the address and I'll come to you.'

'No,' said Lonely. 'I'll come to you. I feel safer on the move, Mr. Callan.'

Callan told him where the park was, and how to get there, said it again, then told the little man to repeat it back to him. It came out with no trouble.

'That's the way, old son,' he said. 'Come on over. I'll hang on till you get here. Only make sure you're not followed.'

There was a gasp from the other end of the phone, and then silence.

Callan said, 'Lonely! Lonely! Are you all right?'

At last Lonely said, 'Yeah. It's O.K. Mr. Callan. See you in the park then?'

'I'll be here,' said Callan.

'It's just that – things have been happening,' said Lonely. 'Me Aunty Gertie's dead.'

222

15

Callan waited, and the time crept by; the park emptied. Mums and nippers going back to tea and telly. Half an hour. Forty-five minutes. Come on Lonely, he thought. If you don't get your skates on they'll close the bloody park. He'd used the same dodge as the last time; taking cover behind a clump of trees that faced a stretch of grassland, but nobody came except two fellers and a bird walking their dogs, because it was an offence to let them foul the pavement, and anyway it made the grass grow... Then he saw the blind man, and thought at once of the day before; of the Groper and Terry – and Amanda. He watched and the blind man came nearer, white-stick feeling its way, dark glasses covering the eyes like stains. The last of the dog-walkers left, and the blind man's stick sought and found the edge of the grass, he stopped on it and moved forward. There was nobody else in sight.

Callan left the shelter of the trees and came up to Lonely, and the little man dropped the stick and took off the glasses.

'I remember you did that the other day,' he said.

'Yesterday,' said Callan.

'Worked for you,' said Lonely, 'so I thought–'

'But they might have been watching you, old son,' said Callan. 'That's why I did it. I didn't want to take any chances.'

Lonely said, 'And for all I knew they might have been watching me. That's why I did it. I didn't want to take no chances either. I reckon I've taken enough.'

You stupid berk, thought Callan. That was the biggest chance of the lot. Don't you realise by now they'll be looking for a blind man? But he didn't say it aloud. Lonely was in no shape for any more shocks.

'You'd better tell me about it,' he said.

Out it all came then, blast and shattered windows and flame, and the frantic scramble back into the house and up the banister rail, to find her broken, disfigured, dead; and not once had it crossed the little man's mind that he had acted bravely. He could talk of nothing but his loss.

'And then what happened?' Callan asked.

'I went out the back,' said Lonely. 'That's how I know I wasn't followed. There wasn't nobody there, Mr. Callan. They was all out the front enjoying the sights.'

'And then?'

'Like I told you,' said Lonely. 'I walked... I walked my bleeding feet off. Barmy thing to do, wasn't it? Maybe I was barmy.'

224

'Shock,' said Callan. 'Not surprising after what you'd been through.'

'I kept seeing her,' said Lonely. 'And then I kept remembering her – the way she used to be like. And then I thought – something ought to be done about them gits that did that to her. And then I remembered I'd promised to call you.'

'You reckon I ought to do something about those gits?'

'I reckon you owe her.'

'I know I do mate,' said Callan. 'But it might not be an easy debt to repay.'

'Her sons is dead,' said Lonely, 'so that leaves me. And I–'

'You did all right, old son,' said Callan. 'If she'd been alive you'd have got her out.'

'But she wasn't alive,' said Lonely. 'She was dead. And if I hadn't come out to 'phone you I'd have been dead too.'

Callan said, 'What you're asking – it isn't easy.'

But Lonely said again, 'You owe her,' and left it at that. So far as he was concerned, that was all there was to it. He didn't know the state Callan's eyes were in and if he had done he probably wouldn't have cared. A debt was a debt, and that was that. Callan remembered the way Aunty Gertie had fed him, her offer of a loan, the healthy enjoyment in her voice when she'd said, 'I do like watching a man shaving.' He owed her, right

225

enough, and he knew it; but the enemy was so strong. Strong enough to hurt and kill again, if he didn't stop them. He looked again at Lonely, patiently waiting, confident that Callan would honour his debts.

'All right,' he said. 'But we'll have to get a gun.'

'We been through all that, Mr. Callan,' Lonely said. 'You know we can't. Anyway – you can manage without a shooter. I've seen you.'

'Not against these fellers.'

'Who are they then?' said Lonely. 'What makes them so special?'

Callan said, 'If I knew who they were it wouldn't be quite so difficult. This is a contract. Blokes brought in from abroad.'

'Foreigners?'

'Yes,' said Callan. By the look on Lonely's face that made it worse. Lonely was the greatest chauvinist he'd ever met.

Callan said, 'Have you got any money?'

'Few quid,' said Lonely. 'And me Post Office book. I got a hundred and thirty eight pound sixteen p in the Post Office.'

'How much you got on you now?'

'There isn't enough to buy you a gun,' said Lonely.

'I'm not thinking about guns,' said Callan. 'I'm thinking about how we're going to live.'

Lonely turned out his pockets. Three pound notes, a handful of pence; then Callan

226

went through his pockets: a couple of quid, a fifty-pence piece, loose change, his keys, a handkerchief, and three long rifle .22 calibre bullets.

'I see you managed to get some ammo,' Lonely said.

Callan looked at the bullets. Long rifle. Marksman's stuff, but then the Woodsman was a marksman's weapon: rifled barrel. Precision instrument. It had to be. Nobody ever used a Woodsman as a stopper. Those .22 bullets either killed you or you hardly noticed you'd been hit.

'Maybe we can get a gun,' he said.

'You know somebody?'

'I know somewhere,' said Callan.

Lonely sighed, and reached for his Post Office book.

'How much, Mr. Callan?' he asked.

'We'll nick it.'

'Do an Army barracks?'

The idea seemed to inspire as much awe as terror.

'Nothing so glamorous,' said Callan. 'We're going to do an office block.'

'Tonight?'

Callan shook his head. This one was going to take time – and a hell of a lot of talk. There was a lot of danger in it for Lonely.

'Tomorrow,' he said. 'Let's think about where we're going to eat and kip.'

'I have been thinking about it,' said Lonely.

227

'I don't see it's any problem.'

'No problem?' said Callan. 'We haven't six quid between us.'

'There's plenty caffs,' said Lonely.

'Oh sure. We grab a bite at the Mirabelle then book into the Savoy I suppose?'

Lonely sighed. For such a clever geezer Mr. Callan could sometimes be incredibly stupid.

'We find an empty house,' he said. 'Break in and kip. Cost us nothing – we even show a bit of profit.'

'No thieving,' said Callan. 'We sleep there and that's all.'

'You just said you were going to nick a gun.'

'And that's all I'm going to nick,' said Callan. 'Ever.'

'You'd sooner bloody starve I suppose?'

'If I don't nick that gun I may have to,' said Callan. 'If I'm lucky.'

'All right then,' said Lonely, resigned. 'Let's go and eat.'

His judgement in cheap caffs was unerring, and he found one almost at once. The food was neither better nor worse than that of the others Callan had used, but the quantities they served were enormous. After they'd eaten they strolled about the streets, and Lonely looked out for an empty house.

'Good time of year for this lark, Mr. Callan,' he said. 'Summer coming on. People taking a bit of a holiday. Only we don't want to kip round here. We may as well make ourselves comfortable.'

They walked on until the shops grew more affluent, the houses became detached from each other, with gardens front and back.

'This is more like it,' Lonely said. 'Hold on a minute.'

He stopped by a shallow wall enclosing a house with a neat and well-stocked garden. Set into indentations in the wall were clumps of soil, and in them flowers grew. Lonely stooped to tie his shoelace, and when he stood up he had a bunch of violets. He walked on.

'All we need now's a bit of wrapping,' he said.

He found that in a litter-bin.

'I like this kind of neighbourhood,' said Lonely. 'Everybody's so nice and tidy – and reliable.' As he spoke he wrapped the violets in paper. 'Just take a look at the name of the road,' he said, and looked at the sign. 'Laburnum Lane. Classy that is... Now you wait here, Mr. Callan. There's one in the street we just left.'

'Marigold Lane?'

'That's right.'

'How do you know?'

'The garden's nice but the grass needs cutting,' said Lonely. 'And they've drawn all the upstairs curtains – woman that would be. House-proud. Doesn't want anybody looking in – and there's a newspaper stuck in the door. They're away all right.'

'And if you're wrong I suppose you give them the flowers and apologise?'

'If I'm wrong I say I've been asked to deliver these and I must have got the wrong address. Make out like I'm looking for Laburnum Lane.'

'And if you're right?'

'I ring and ring and hope to God I get a nosy neighbour.'

'You want to be seen?'

'He won't remember what I look like,' said Lonely. 'People never do. All he'll say is they're away, and I'll ask him if it's Laburnum Lane and he'll think I'm a berk because everybody knows it's Marigold Lane. So he goes off laughing and so do I because I know the place is empty.'

'You're not just a pretty face are you?' said Callan.

Lonely smirked. 'I have me moments,' he said. 'Now you just wait there by that bus stop, Mr. Callan, and leave it all to me.'

Callan waited, and Lonely came back at last, and tidily dropped the violets in a litter-bin.

'Did it work?' Callan asked.

'Just like I said. Except it was a nosy old bird, not a feller. They've gone to Majorca for a fortnight – back next Saturday. Now you and me'll find a nice pub and wait till it gets dark.'

When they came back Marigold Lane had gone to bed for the most part, and Lonely moved like a shadow down the path to the house, Callan behind him. He passed the front door and windows that were open to the lights of the street, and moved round to the back. The back door he knew would be locked and bolted – people never went away on holiday without locking and bolting the back door, but sometimes they did other things equally barmy. Like this geezer for instance. He'd gone and left the top larder window open. On account of it was too small for people to climb in by. But if you stood on the window sill and pulled the top window down further you could unlatch the bottom window. And maybe the happy house-owner thinks this one's too small an' all, thought Lonely. But to get into a gaff like this you have to be a bit of a contortionist. He eased his body neatly and precisely into the confining space, and a minute later opened the back door to Callan. Throughout the time Callan, listening intently, had not heard a sound. They went into the kitchen, and Lonely carefully drew the blinds close, then struck a match and opened a kitchen cupboard.

'Make yourself at home, Mr. Callan,' he said.

Callan watched as Lonely hunted, struck more matches, and found a candle and a saucer, shielded the candle's light from the window with a bread board, then looked around him.

'Not bad,' he said. 'Mind you I prefer open plan meself.'

Using his handkerchief, he opened cupboards, freezer, refrigerator.

'We should have saved our money,' he said. 'There's a stack of stuff here. Look at this. Pheasant in wine sauce. Wonder what it'd be like cold?' He looked round for a tin-opener.

'Terrible,' said Callan. 'Put it back.'

'All right if I make a brew of tea?' Callan nodded. 'I thought it would. Tea's not thieving. Down and outs always gets tea.'

He filled the kettle, put it on the stove, then went out to explore, and was back just in time to make the tea, find sugar and condensed milk.

'Very comfortable, Mr. Callan,' he said. 'Very comfortable indeed. Belongs to a chartered accountant.'

'How on earth do you know?'

'Got a picture of himself getting his diploma. Couple of nice daughters. One of them takes riding lessons. Wife's not bad-looking either – if you like them skinny. Twin beds though. When you're married that's ridiculous. If they'd bought a double it might have

232

put a bit of meat on her.' He poured the tea. 'Still it means you and me'll be comfortable.' He yawned. 'Think I'll take this up with me. We've got to make an early start tomorrow.'

'I think we better talk first,' said Callan.

'What about?'

'We've got another job to do tomorrow.'

'Nicking a gun,' said Lonely. 'I hadn't forgotten. You got a gunsmith's lined up in that office block, Mr. Callan?'

'No,' said Callan. 'Not a gunsmith's. They're never easy, and we mightn't get a handgun anyway. You just sit there and drink your tea, old son. There's a bit more to this than just nicking a gun, so I want you to know what you're in for.'

When he had done, Lonely said: 'I don't think I can.'

'Take your time,' said Callan. 'Think about it. You owe her something too – and I can't do it without you.'

'Suppose it goes wrong, Mr. Callan?'

'Then we both die,' said Callan.

'Gawd,' Lonely said. 'How can you just sit there and say that?'

'Maybe I don't have all that much to live for.'

'Maybe I don't either,' said Lonely. 'But I'm a coward, Mr. Callan. I always was.'

'You'll be all right if you do what I'm telling you,' said Callan. No answer. 'I won't miss, old son. Shooting's my business – and

I'm good at it.' Still no answer. 'All right,' he said. 'Sleep on it. Tell me in the morning.'

Lonely said, 'I'm stinking, aren't I?'

Callan said, 'I didn't say so.'

'You didn't have to. Funny, innit? When I climbed in to get Aunty – all that – I was fresh as a vase full of roses. And now I niff just thinking about it.'

'Don't think about it.'

'Mr Callan, how can I help it?' said Lonely. He went upstairs to take a bath.

Callan woke before daylight. The bed was warm and the darkness relaxing, and he got up at once before sleep came back to him, then called softly to Lonely, but his bed was empty. He made his way downstairs and into the kitchen, and there the little man sat, haggard and miserable, drinking tea by candle-light: but it didn't look much like gracious living.

'I couldn't sleep, Mr. Callan,' he said, 'so I got up and made a brew. Want some?'

Callan yawned and nodded, and Lonely poured out tea, hands trembling so much that it slopped into the saucer.

'I'm going to do it,' Lonely said. Callan looked at him.

'You're sure?' he asked.

'Gawd blimey,' said Lonely. 'Is that all I get? Not even a thank you?'

'That's more like it,' said Callan. 'Thanks

234

me old son.' He drank his tea. 'We'd better be going.'

'I'll just rinse the cups,' said Lonely. Callan stared at him.

'Well,' Lonely said, 'so long as we're not going to nick anything we may as well leave the place tidy. This is a respectable neighbourhood.' He even remembered to lock the pantry window, then put on his coat and cap. He was ready.

'Going out's when we got to be careful,' he said. 'We don't look nothing like so respectable as the neighbourhood, and rozzers gets nosy about things like that. We'll be all right when we get to that street where the caff is, because there we'll be working men going on early shift – but round here we better keep our eyes open.'

Callan thought, There's nothing I'd like better. Because if my eyes aren't working properly, this whole caper's off.

Aloud he said, 'You're the expert,' and Lonely gave the smirk of one to whom such praise is due, and led the way.

He set off in the familiar scurrying run, and Callan had to hurry to keep up with him, as he moved through side streets and zig-zagged his way to the point where Callan was hopelessly lost, but Lonely moved through the district as if he'd grown up in it. Only once did they see a policeman, but he didn't see them. Lonely touched Callan's shoulder and they moved into a garden, crouched behind a hedge till he went past. Then afterwards they saw no one at all until they reached the shops.

'The only good thing about coppers is there's not all that many of them,' said Lonely.

Once past the shops, the people appeared. Men for the most part, walking singly or in pairs, and the occasional woman off to do some office cleaning. Men and women alike walked in a kind of angry slouch as they faced another day's work.

'Poor bastards,' said Lonely. 'I wonder how many of them would change places with us if they had the chance?'

When they reached the caff, it was closed. Lonely shrugged.

'I wasn't hungry anyway,' he said.

'You'll eat,' said Callan. 'You can't do a job like this if you don't.'

'I'm beginning to wonder if I can do it at all.'

'That's because you need food,' Callan said. 'Come on and find another caff.'

And Lonely found one the way a gun dog finds a game-bird, and Callan hustled him inside to the familiar atmosphere of steam, cigarette smoke and hot grease. A few men in working clothes sat there, men whose work had just finished, or was just about to begin. Mostly they ate in silence. On the radio a disc jockey rattled off his own brand of happiness. Even the tone of his voice was a mockery.

Callan ordered eggs, bacon and fried bread, and Lonely polished his off before Callan had half-finished.

'I thought you weren't hungry,' he said.

'I thought I wasn't,' said Lonely. He looked round the caff: scarred chairs and tables, walls covered in advertisements for soft drinks, most of them defaced, the cigarette machine marked 'Out of Order'.

'I reckon it's the atmosphere in this place,' he said. 'It sort of relaxes you.'

Callan brought him more tea.

'What now?' said Lonely.

'We wait,' said Callan.

'I hate the waiting.'

'Everybody does,' Callan said. 'You get used to it.'

Lonely looked up, stared into Callan's eyes. They were flat, and somehow empty. They told you nothing.

'You really have done this before,' he said.

'I told you.'

'Yeah I know but – I never knew you was like that.'

'Like what?' said Callan.

'Like you're used to it.'

Callan said, 'We better find a place where we can shave.'

'Shave?' said Lonely. 'Blimey have you

gone barmy?'

'These geezers know me,' said Callan. 'They know everything about me. That means they know I shave every day – no matter what. So we'll shave.'

'We better go to a station then,' said Lonely. 'Find a Wash and Brush Up place.'

'Fine,' said Callan. 'It'll help to pass the time.'

Lonely shuddered.

16

They went to Charing Cross, and by that time Lonely's hand had started to shake again so much that Callan had to shave him as well as himself.

'I never knew you had to be so particular just to get shot,' said Lonely.

'I'll be doing the shooting,' said Callan, '–and it won't be at you.'

Maybe, he thought. If nothing goes wrong. If they don't grab Lonely too soon, and Lonely doesn't panic, and if my eyes stay as good as they are now – then maybe. And then again, maybe not. He took Lonely to a post office then, and made him take ten pounds out of his account. It was like pulling ten teeth. After that they had to find a shoe-shop that sold platform shoes, and Lonely had to cough up most of the ten quid. He went on about that, too, and about the fact that Callan made him practise wearing them when his feet were so sore: but at least it helped to keep his mind off what lay ahead.

'I'll never look like you,' said Lonely.

'You're looking more like me all the time,' Callan said. 'Look how tall you've grown.'

'Me feet's just two big blisters.'

'Let's go and sit down and rest them.'

It was like that all day; Callan patiently, kindly sustaining Lonely's morale, that was about as frail as his Aunty Glad's virtue. They had beer and sandwiches at lunch time, then took a bus to Hyde Park, where Lonely sat and worried in the sunshine, and Callan dozed in the shade. Then suddenly he was awake, every nerve telling him it was time to move.

'I reckon it's about time, old son,' he said.

'Oh my Gawd,' said Lonely.

'Are you still sure?'

'I been thinking about Aunty Gertie,' Lonely said. 'I got to do it, Mr. Callan.'

'She'd be proud of you,' said Callan.

This time Lonely didn't smirk, but it made him feel better.

Callan picked up Lonely's raincoat, took the cap from Lonely's head, and put them on. The cap just about fitted, the raincoat didn't; but then it hadn't fitted Lonely either. Lonely stood up then, and put on Callan's overcoat and hat. The hat came down over his ears, and they had to line it with newspaper. The overcoat wasn't too bad, thanks to the built-up shoes. After that all they had to do was walk to Swan and Edgar's and buy three feet of white curtain rail, and a large buff envelope that Callan filled out with the rest of the newspaper. Then they were ready, and Callan walked with Lonely down to the tube and watched him buy his ticket.

'Now remember,' he said. 'Stay in sight of other people. All the time.'

'Yes, Mr. Callan.'

'And when you get to the building, don't go into the lift on your own. And when you get to that corridor I told you about – move.'

'Yes, Mr. Callan.'

'And when I call out to you, do exactly as I tell you. It'll be just the way I told you about it.'

'No it won't Mr. Callan.'

Callan smiled. 'Well maybe not exactly,' he said, 'but at least by that time it'll be nearly over... Good luck, old son.'

'And to you, Mr. Callan.' The little man hesitated. 'Suppose they aren't there?' he said at last.

'They'll be there,' said Callan.

'But what makes you so sure?'

'I told you,' said Callan. 'They know me. They know me inside out. That means they know I'll come looking for you – once I've read about the accident. And when I come looking, they'll be waiting.'

Lonely sighed. 'I'd better be off then,' he said and walked through the barrier, negotiated the escalator with his platform shoes, and disappeared from sight. The last Callan saw of him was his hat.

Callan bought his own tube ticket then, and while he waited for the train he thought of the name to write on the envelope that was going to be his passport to the vast, unlovely office block. No commissionaire would stop him delivering a letter to somebody who worked there, especially if that somebody had a bit of class, he thought. Bloke with his own office and secretary. 'H. Remington Bissett, Esq.' Callan wrote, then added 'C.B.E.'. Below that he wrote, 'Sales Division', then in the left hand corner, 'By Hand. Urgent'. The cap bothered him. It was too tight, and being Lonely's, a bit niffy. Callan took it off and stowed it carefully in a raincoat pocket as the train came in. Lonely was very fond of that cap. Callan took off the raincoat then, and folded it over his arm. If he'd refused to put them on while Lonely was there he'd have hurt the little man's feelings, and he had enough problems with Lonely as it was.

His mate. His mucker. The little man who'd found courage in grief, and dignity, too. 'I reckon you owe her.' There'd been dignity in that, and he, Callan, had respected it – or pretended to. Because it wasn't that simple; not really. He'd needed Lonely all along, and used him: to try for a gun, to find him a doctor, and now he needed him as a decoy; not for Aunty Gertie; for himself. Revenge was a stupid business; all unnecessary killing was stupid. All it did was increase your risks without any compensatory gains. But this kill

242

wasn't for revenge. This one had the promise of tremendous gains that justified all the risks he was taking: one more enemy dead and a gun for Callan. It didn't justify the risks that Lonely was taking, or the gratitude that he would feel if Callan brought it off. But at least Lonely would have had his revenge, and Callan would be one step nearer doing something about Amanda... Amanda and Lonely. Beauty and the Beast. And both at risk.

His train reached its station and he moved in the ant-swarm that flowed up the escalator and out into the street; jostling, being jostled by the other descending swarm that moved with the cheerful vigour of men and women for whom the day's work is over, till he reached the office-block. Palatine House. Headquarters of the world's seventh largest conglomerate: steel, copper, zinc, silver, plastics. Shipping too, and canned foods and electronics. They even owned a few pop-groups. Worldwide interests. Hong Kong, South America, the Canadian Arctic – and they ran the lot from this monstrous great sprawl on the bank of the Thames; thousands of offices, miles of corridors, millions of pounds. It held as many people as a fair-sized town, and like a town it provided for all their needs: it fed them, sheltered them, gave them work and entertainment. It could find beds for them, give them haircuts, manicures, beauty treatments, games and exercise. One day, Callan thought, the people who worked there might never be allowed to go outside. They might not even want to.

He remembered the job he'd done there. They'd been developing a heat-resistant plastic, and the Ministry of Defence was interested because a heat-resistant plastic was just what was needed for rockets – and East Germany had been interested too, and Egypt. Because heat-resistant plastic would help their rockets go bang. There'd been a leak, just a small one, but Hunter had been afraid it might grow bigger, so Callan had gone along on standby; just in case the East Germans or the Egyptians sent along a few heavies. But Special Branch had plugged the leak before it had time to grow and arrested the poor bastard who had caused it: Robson was it? Robinson? Dobson? and had sent him to prison: a dazed little commuter with a mortgage and a marriage that had both turned dodgy. And H. Remington Bissett had been the one who'd first spotted the leak, hence, presumably, the C.B.E.

Robson – Robinson – Dobson had looked as if he'd really signed on for life: member of so many clubs and organisations you'd wonder he ever had time to go home to his wife – or his mortgage; but in the end he'd rebelled; bit the hand that fed him, betrayed the firm. And that was what had appalled Bissett: that one of his division had been guilty of *disloyalty*. To the firm. Disloyalty to his country had come a lot lower down Bissett's list. But he'd been a man who was easily appalled, Callan remembered. Anything that showed ignorance of the firm appalled him: like how big Palatine House was, and how many recreational facilities – he loved words like recreational facilities – and went on and on about squash courts and swimming baths and rifle clubs and gymnasiums and the best-equipped amateur theatre in the country. What a boring bastard he had been. Maybe that was why Callan had forgotten Palatine House. Boredom had almost wiped it from his memory; that and the tears of the poor bloody commuter when the Special Branch Inspector started reciting the charge...

He walked briskly towards the great rank of doors, through one marked 'In'. Another great swarm of workers surged past him through the 'Out' doors, let off on parole until the next morning. The vast foyer was crowded with other potential escapers, and the four commissionaires on duty looked on like benevolent gaolers. Callan moved into the crowd, an ant in an army of ants, up to the vast indicator board, and nobody bothered. He found the place with no trouble at all – 7 Green corridor, J4 and 5, and moved to the lifts. Another squad of prisoners came out, and Callan and a few more got in, and still nobody bothered. He had an envelope with a name on it, and so presumably he was going to deliver it and who the hell cared? Certainly not the ones who were still confined to Palatine House when everybody else was going home.

He got out at floor seven and walked down the green corridor, not hurrying, because other people were walking down it too, but when he turned into the off-shoot marked J there was no-one in sight, and he could risk hurrying. The door might take time, even with his keys. The fact that it didn't, he thought, was because Bartram's had supplied the locks, and Bartram's were the people he'd once worked for. It took him seventeen seconds to get inside. Then he could risk a light, turn his attention to a slender, steel-lined case that stood against one wall. Bartram's had made that one too, but it might be a bit more tricky than the door. All the same, he knew he could do it in a quarter of the time he had. Then all he had to do was wait. After that it was up to Lonely.

It was all very well Mr. Callan saying stay in the crowd, but there wasn't any crowd round the market this time of night, just a lot of stall-holders who'd spot him like a shot if he got too close, even with his built-up shoes and his white stick. Think he'd gone barmy, they would. *And* talk about it. He looked through his dark glasses to the coffee-bar, Aunty Gertie's coffee-bar. Closed up for good now, and nobody hanging round it that he could see. Better keep moving. He tap-tapped his way through the maze of streets that he knew so well, heading towards the house where his gaff had been, before those gits blew it apart. Not right up to it – that would have been stupid, what with all the people who knew him, and all wondering where he'd got to – but just as far as the corner; slow and taking his time because Mr. Callan had told him, over and over he'd told him, to remember he was blind and use his stick.

The sight of the house shattered him. He hadn't seen anything like it since the war – a great gaping hole where once his room had been, and what was left all naked for the world to see, the shattered remnants of his furniture, the remains of the wallpaper flapping like tattered banners. All miserable it looked. Grotty. Poor. But it hadn't been like that – not when he lived in it. And especially not when Aunty Gertie had cleaned it up... You've gone far enough now, he told himself. Turn off at the next corner– Then go back to Mr. Callan and tell him it didn't work. And maybe that's just as well for you, he thought, the state your nerves are in.

He turned off and kept going, and suddenly he knew that somebody was on to him. He couldn't look round because blind men don't look round – and anyway if he had it would have been a dead giveaway, but somebody was on to him all right, and Lonely could taste the metal of fear in his mouth, the stinking fear that had gripped him all his life, only this was the worst one ever, and no Aunty Gertie to help him. The only help he had was what Mr. Callan had told him, and he chanted it over to himself as if it were a Talisman. Head straight for a street with people in it. No trouble about that, not with this bastard behind him, not the way he knew the streets round here. Keep on going till you find a place where you can stop being blind.

'How am I going to do that, Mr. Callan?'

Lonely remembered the patient look, the willed and weary patience of a man who was almost down to his last resources of strength. He remembered also what he'd said. Word for word he remembered.

'Find a pub, a shop, a tube-station. Anywhere there's a lot of people. Always make sure there's people – then duck down behind somewhere, take your glasses off. And don't carry that curtain rod like a stick any more. Carry it like a curtain rod.' All right. He could do that too. There was a hotel coming up. Nice old place, dark leather and all that. And two ways in. One was revolving doors, the others you just pushed open. This time of night there'd be bound to be people about because of the cocktail bar. Not that he ever used it, the prices they charged.

He went up to the revolving doors, and pushed. As they moved round, he took off the dark glasses, shifted his grip on the stick, then walked over to the cocktail bar and looked in, a man with a bit of carpentry lined up for the evening, seeing if he could spot a friend... Never in his life had he wanted a drink so desperately, but Lonely knew that if he stopped now he would panic, and anyway Mr. Callan had said for him to keep moving. He remembered the next instructions.

'Keep on going. But make sure he doesn't lose you.'

That was the hard part. Every nerve in Lonely's body screamed at him to take evasive action, and he could have done it too. Nothing easier when it was just a question of a single tail, Lonely knew he could lose anybody. But where was the point in that? It would put you back where you started.

He turned away from the cocktail bar – a bloke whose friend wasn't there – and went out to the street through the other doors. Well at least he could move a bit faster now he wasn't supposed to be blind – but not too fast, in case the git lost him. Get to the bus stop, that was the thing, and wait there in the queue, then see who stands behind him. But when he tried it, the git was too fly. It was two schoolgirls who stood behind him, and a couple of old birds off home to cook their old men's suppers behind them. For a moment Lonely panicked at the thought that he'd imagined the whole thing, that he'd have to do it all again. But he knew that wasn't on. He'd been followed all right, he knew it. It was just that the geezer was good. Or maybe he'd spotted him properly. Knew he wasn't Mr. Callan. Keep your hat pulled down, Mr. Callan had said. Keep your scarf round your face. Well he'd done all that, and he was wearing a sticking plaster just like Mr. Callan was. It wouldn't be his fault if the feller had recognised him.

Then his bus came, and Lonely realised he was still at risk. As he got on a man came running and leaped aboard as the bus moved off. He moved straight past Lonely and went inside as Lonely waited to climb upstairs into the smoky, comforting fog on top. Neither man looked at the other, and yet in the second it took for the man to pass by him, Lonely knew who he was. Biggish geezer, not massive, but with a look of solid power. The kind of look Mr. Callan had. And good at shadowing. Better than good. Look at the way he'd gone downstairs. Lonely would have bet all he possessed that this man would be on one of the side seats nearest to the exit. That way he could pick Lonely up the minute he left the bus, and if he hadn't sensed him already, he wouldn't even know he was being followed. Clever that was, the murdering git. The conductor came up and Lonely handed over his money.

'Palatine House please,' he said.

It didn't take anything like as long as he'd hoped it would. Every day in London they had traffic-jams, hold-ups, but not this day. This day the bus zipped along like it was setting a new record, and they reached the river in no time. They didn't even have to wait to cross the bridge. Lonely remembered his instructions, and pulled down his hat, wrapped the scarf over his face until it covered his mouth. Like he had the bleeding toothache. About all that showed was the scar.

'Get up in good time,' Mr. Callan had said. 'Let him see what stop you're getting off at.'

Heart thumping, knees shaking, Lonely did that too. But the man who was following him was too well trained to get up at once. There were three more people between him and Lonely when they at last left the bus.

Try as he would Lonely couldn't stop himself from hurrying, not this time. The fear was too great. But as he crossed the road to the monstrous building he did have one piece of luck. Three vast Mercedes drew up by the doors and a whole lot of rich geezers got out. The commissionaires were too busy opening car-doors to worry about Lonely. He went inside and the indicator was there exactly where Mr. Callan had said it would be, and there was the place he had to go to: 7 Green Corridor, J4 and 5. Lonely got in the lift, and some of the rich geezers got in with him, and so did the man who was following him. Cautiously Lonely manoeuvred himself so that the rich geezers were between him and his tail, then one of them leaned across to press the top-floor button, sniffed, and moved closer to his mates.

Lonely thought, 'Yes mate, and so would you niff if you had to face what I'm facing. It isn't a bloody cocktail party I'm going to.' He reached out and pressed the seventh floor button as the lift-gates closed. His legs were trembling more violently than ever. He was about to face the worst minutes of his life, and he knew it.

As the gates slid open at the seventh floor he was already moving, scattering the rich geezers right and left. They weren't used to it and they didn't like it, and a fat lot Lonely cared. He'd bumped them into the feller that was tailing him, and that gave him a few seconds' start, and he needed it to find the side corridor marked J. The bloody green corridor seemed about ten miles long, and as empty as the Sahara. He made himself walk as far as C corridor, but then he couldn't help himself; he had to run. From the sounds behind him he knew that the git was running too, and Lonely ran faster till J corridor came up at last and he darted round the corner, doubling like a hare to the door marked four and five. But the bloke behind him was even faster than he was. No time to close the door on him, even if he'd been allowed to. He ran through the door into darkness, and his pursuer followed, still gaining on him. Suddenly the darkness became a blaze of light.

Callan's voice yelled, 'Lonely. Down!' and Lonely dropped as the man behind him whirled, gun in hand, to the direction of the sound. Lonely heard two sharp reports, no louder than whip cracks, and the man who'd followed him reacted as if somebody had thumped him, no more than that, but Lonely could see the small, neat hole in his forehead, the spreading stain of blood on the white shirt. The man seemed to take a long time falling, but Lonely was in no doubt that he was dead.

He looked around for Callan, and saw him rise up from behind a narrow steel cabinet laid on its side. In his hands there was a rifle, a puny-looking little thing that looked like the kind kids use when they play cowboys, but Lonely knew what it had done.

'Oh my Gawd,' he said.

'You all right, old son?'

'It's me legs,' Lonely said. 'They don't seem to do what I tell them.'

253

'Just take it easy,' Callan said. 'Take your time.'

He pushed the door shut, then went up to the dead man, put down the rifle, picked up the dead man's gun. Not a Makarov after all.

'Walther automatic,' he said. 'German. Not the kind I'm used to, but it'll do. The Germans never made a bad gun yet.'

He stuck it in his pants' waistband, then began to go through the dead man's pockets.

'Take my time,' said Lonely. 'We got to get out of here. You just killed a man.'

'This corridor's empty,' Callan said. 'And a .22 doesn't make much noise.'

'Somebody might have heard you.'

'It's possible.'

'Well then—'

Callan said, 'This is a miniature rifle range. I told you. People expect to hear shooting.'

'All the same we ought to scarper. Suppose somebody comes in?'

'Nobody'll come in,' said Callan. 'Didn't you see the notice on the door?'

'I didn't have time to hang about reading notices.'

Callan looked up at him then. Poor little bastard, he was terrified out of his mind. 'All right,' said Callan. 'We'll scarper.'

Lonely moved off like a shot.

'No,' said Callan. 'Not like that.' He began to stow the dead man's possessions into his

254

own pockets. 'We go out like respectable people,' he said.

'So long as we go,' said Lonely, and moved off again. Callan picked up the rifle, ejected the one remaining long .22 shell, then wiped the rifle carefully. When he had finished he tossed up the .22 shell, caught it and put it in his pocket. It was as good a souvenir as any. When he followed Lonely out, he didn't look at the dead man.

'You wasn't in a hurry, was you?' Lonely said.

Callan said, 'I was giving you time to read the notice.'

He nodded at the door. Held there by a thumb-tack was a white card with a skull and cross bones on it, painted in red, and below, in neat red lettering: 'Danger. Firing in Progress. Keep Out.'

'You mean to say you didn't see that?' Callan asked.

Lonely said, 'I was lucky to see the bleeding door.'

Callan closed the door then, and heard the lock click. It wouldn't do for the dead man to be found before they'd left.

They took the lift to the first floor, and from there they used a fire-escape that brought them out to a vast, empty yard filled with cars. There was a bloke on duty by the yard gate, and Lonely wanted to run for it, but Callan held him back and they walked out nice and easy. Callan even called out 'Goodnight.' Not that the bloke on duty answered, but at least he didn't try to stop them. When they were outside, Callan looked again at Lonely.

'I think you'd better have a drink,' he said.

'I know I better,' said Lonely.

17

They found a pub that was quiet, and Callan bought two whiskies, large ones.

'I don't like that stuff, Mr. Callan,' Lonely said.

'Get it down you.'

Lonely sipped and shuddered, and found that just for once it wasn't so bad after all.

'You did all right,' said Callan.

'I was scared all the time.'

'You had a good right to be,' said Callan.

'You wasn't scared,' said Lonely.

Callan said, 'I had the easy job.'

'Anyway,' said Lonely, 'we showed them.'

'We did,' said Callan. 'Give me a bit of cover will you?'

Lonely twisted in his chair so that his body was between Callan and the view from the bar.

The first thing Callan looked at was a knife, needle-pointed, its cutting edge razor sharp, in a worn, plain leather sheath.

'Looks like we did this job for Terry and the Groper as well,' said Callan. He stowed it away and took out the next item: a piece of bright yellow plastic, round in shape, about the size of a button.

Callan said, 'This geezer's the one that killed your aunty, all right.'

Lonely said, 'What makes you so sure?'

'This.' Callan held up the button and put it back in his pocket.

'That's a plastic detonator, old son.'

'Murdering git,' said Lonely.

'And that's about it,' said Callan. 'A knife, a detonator, and a Walther automatic. And money.' He took it out and began to count it. 'Quite a lot of money.' Tenners, fivers, and a fistful of pound notes – over a hundred quid. Some of the pound notes were new, a paper wrapper still round them. Written on the wrapper was a phone number, and an extension. And that should have been a clue, thought Callan, except that he knew the number – it was the hospital, and the extension, it was the ophthalmic surgeon's. Just as well he'd decided to play blind man's buff. Below the telephone number was a street plan, crudely drawn, the streets unnamed, and yet somehow those streets made sense to Callan, he knew he had walked them. He looked again at the hospital number, and suddenly he remembered. He put the wrapper in his pocket and counted the money more carefully, divided by two, and pushed half over to Lonely.

'I thought you didn't do no thieving,' Lonely said.

'This isn't thieving,' said Callan. 'This is

258

spoils of war.'

He waited, but Lonely made no move to pick it up.

'What's the matter with you?' Callan asked. 'Take it.'

'I don't want it,' Lonely said, then– 'You killed that geezer.'

'*We* killed him,' said Callan. 'You set him up and I knocked him over.'

'It doesn't seem right – robbing a dead man.'

'It didn't seem right to blow up your aunty,' Callan said. 'What's made you so moral all of a sudden?'

Lonely said, 'I never seen anybody killed before. The way you go on, you'd think it was nothing.'

'Maybe rat-catchers feel the same way,' said Callan. 'Look – you wanted us to do it. You said we both owed her – and I agreed. Right? So we did it, and it's finished. Full stop. So belt up.'

He shoved the money into Lonely's pocket.

Lonely said, 'It isn't finished, Mr. Callan. You said there were two of them – and we only got one.'

Callan said, 'I don't understand you. I really don't. First you get a conscience for the first time in your life – and now you're getting greedy.'

'All I meant was he'll know it was us that done it. So now he'll be after both of us.'

'Yeah – only this time I've got a gun.'

'I haven't,' said Lonely. He drank more whisky. The fear was receding now, and in its place came bewilderment.

'And I don't want one neither.' He drank again. 'I seen a man killed. I don't want to see another.'

'You better leave it to me then,' Callan said.

'What'll I do?'

'Find a place to kip and stay out of trouble.'

'It'll be a pleasure,' said Lonely.

Komorowski, he thought. Better put him in the picture. After all, he did give me a good dinner. So he went up West, and walked to the Mews. The car wasn't there, but that didn't matter. He could wait. Now that he had a gun, there was no harm in waiting. It gave him a chance to think, about his bird and Lonely and the dead man. It was funny about the dead man: he'd never even got a proper look at him until he was dead. And then it was just a face he'd never seen before, a face that had been shipped a thousand miles to do a bit of shooting, and ended up by being shot himself. He'd been good though; fast and quick-thinking, right up to that last impossible moment. A knife, a detonator and a pistol. A walking bloody arsenal. But no heart; arsenals don't need them...

The Rolls purred by, and Callan watched

from a doorway as the garage doors swung open and the car moved forward. Callan crossed the street and walked behind the Rolls's offside wheel into the garage, his coat open, the butt of the pistol visible, as the garage door swung shut behind him. Two people in the car – Komorowski, and Lonely's Aunty Glad. It would be nice to give her news of her nephew. Komorowski got out first, and Callan moved from behind the car into the light.

'Evening,' he said.

Komorowski reacted as if he'd been prodded with a spike. The first thing he saw was the gun.

'Yeah,' said Callan. 'I finally got one. Evening, Miss de Courcy Mannering.'

'Cut that out for a start,' she said.

Komorowski said, 'What may I do for you, Mr. Callan?'

'Bit of a chat,' Callan said.

Komorowski made an eloquent gesture of acceptance. The last of the ancien régime, thought Callan, then he spoiled it all by leading the way.

'Come, come,' said Callan. 'Ladies first.'

Aunty Glad swept up the stairs like a duchess.

The room was opulent and warm as always, a token of the kind of place he would have had himself, if he'd used the gun to get it. Callan waited as Komorowski sat behind the desk, and Aunty Glad sank gracefully into a vast and welcoming armchair. Callan himself remained standing, hands loose at his sides, the gun-butt clearly visible, and watched Komorowski, who sat like a stone man.

'I bet I know what you're thinking about,' said Callan.

'I didn't come up here to play guessing games,' Aunty Glad said.

Komorowski said, 'Belt up,' but his eyes never left Callan. 'What am I thinking about?'

'You're thinking about the gun in your desk drawer – and how you're going to get it before I get mine. The answer's easy. You're not.'

His hand moved then, and the gun was there, its one unblinking eye looking at Komorowski's head.

'Get away from the desk,' said Callan, and Komorowski obeyed. 'And pour us all a drink. I thought you aristocrats were supposed to be hospitable.' He went to the desk. 'Scotch for me.'

Komorowski went over to the drinks table, and Callan pulled open the desk drawer. As he glanced into it, Aunty Glad stood up, and the gun's eye stared at her, hard and un-wavering.

'No,' said Callan.

'Don't be foolish Gladys,' Komorowski

said, and poured her a gin and tonic. She sat down again, and Callan reached into the drawer, took out a revolver.

'Well, well,' he said. 'Just what I always wanted. A Smith and Wesson .38 Magnum. You won't mind if I borrow it for a while, will you?'

He put the Walther in his pocket, and picked up the revolver instead. Komorowski made the acquiescent gesture again.

'What will you take with your Scotch?' he asked.

'Your Scotch I'll take neat,' Callan said. 'Pour your own and sit beside Miss de Courcy Mannering.'

Aunty Glad said, 'You stop calling me that.'

'I could call you a lot worse,' said Callan, 'if I wanted.'

Komorowski sighed.

'You set me up,' Callan said. 'You and the Count here.'

'You're barmy,' she said.

'You got a young queen's face slashed so he looks like a patchwork quilt, from what I hear – and you got your sister-in-law killed.'

'Gertie?'

'Gertie. You would have got Lonely killed too – if he hadn't gone out.'

'I had nothing to do with it.'

Callan drank his Scotch left-handed, and looked at Komorowski.

'And you?'

'I offered you a job,' Komorowski said, 'and you refused it.'

'So you shopped me?'

'You appear to think so.'

'I know so. There was only one way anybody could know I was going to see the Groper—'

'I have never heard of such a person.'

'Maybe you haven't,' said Callan. 'That isn't the point. You persuaded Miss de Courcy Mannering here to let someone bug her phone.'

'She couldn't have done this without me?'

Aunty Glad looked at him with distaste.

'She could have,' Callan said. 'But I don't think she would. She's very respectable nowadays, you know. Not the sort to get mixed up in anything vulgar, like slashing a feller, or blowing up a middle-aged woman. Not unless you made her.'

'And how would I do that?'

'By having something on her – just as they had something on you.'

'The mysterious "they",' Komorowski said. 'Just who are they supposed to be?'

'The K.G.B,' said Callan.

Aunty Glad said, 'I don't hold with politics. Never have.'

'Then you shouldn't get mixed up with politicians,' said Callan. He turned to Komorowski. 'What did they use on you?' There

264

was no answer. 'Your mother?' Komorowski nodded.

'If I helped them they swore she would have honourable treatment,' he said. 'If not–'

Callan said, 'You don't have to draw any pictures.'

'It was not an easy decision to make,' Komorowski said. 'I was after all indebted to you – I still am. That was why I offered you the job. If you had taken it–'

'They'd have punished your mother.'

'I have not seen her for thirty-four years,' Komorowski said. 'It was not an easy decision to make.'

'Until I turned you down. Don't talk to me about debts, mate. What you wanted was a gunman. Me. When you didn't get me, you didn't give a damn, so long as they left you in peace to get on with your business.'

Aunty Glad said, 'I never shopped Gertie.'

'They had a bug on your phone,' said Callan, 'and one in your drawing room. They heard Lonely and me talking. They knew how much I needed him, how much he helped me. And they worked out even more. Because they're clever, Miss de Courcy Mannering. They know all about people – and their little weaknesses, like friendship and loyalty and affection. Maybe you've read about things like that?'

'I wouldn't have hurt Lonely – or Gertie either,' Aunty Glad said.

'They knew if Lonely died I might get mad and come looking for revenge,' Callan said. 'Then they'd have me off-guard and careless, and they'd kill me. Gertie was a bit of bad luck for them – but not too bad. I owed her, too. It still might have worked. I still might have come roaring up for revenge. Do you think anybody would want to avenge your death, Miss de Courcy Mannering?'

Aunty Glad turned to Komorowski.

'You rotten bastard,' she said. 'You never told me about that.' Then the rage died, and she wept.

'Now tell me about Susan Marsden,' Callan said, 'and please don't put on that puzzled look. Not tonight.'

'Glad gets grass for her,' Komorowski said. 'And a little speed, sometimes. That colleague of yours collects it.'

'And where does Glad get it from?' Callan asked.

'From him.' Aunty Glad scowled at Komorowski. Behind her tears, her eyes held nothing but rage. 'Lord Muck. He's far too grand to do his pushing himself. All he does is buy it wholesale. Right, Your Highness?'

'The stupidity business,' said Callan, and looked at Komorowski. 'At one time I thought I was going to kill you.'

'You have changed your mind?'

'You're not worth it,' Callan said. 'You're a cheap gangster – and you belong with all the other cheap gangsters – in the nick. I'm going to shop you.'

'You would find it hard to prove anything.'

'I don't think so,' Callan said. 'We had a file on you – and I still remember quite a bit of it. And there's always Susan Marsden.' He looked at Aunty Glad, still weeping. 'I'm going to shop Miss de Courcy Mannering, too,' he said.

'I never knew what they were going to do to Gertie,' she said. 'Honest.'

'You may be telling the truth,' said Callan. 'But there are other people – like the Marsden girl. And anyway, when I give them the Count here, they're bound to want you as well. After all, you've been together for so long.'

'You can shop us – O.K.,' said Komorowksi. 'But you'll still be dead. Be sensible, Callan. What kind of revenge is that? I've got a better idea.'

'Let's hear it,' said Callan.

'My other offer,' Komorowski said. 'It's still open.'

Callan laughed aloud.

'I'm perfectly serious,' said Komorowski, and rose to his feet. 'Let me show you.' He moved towards a wall-safe. The movement took him closer to Callan.

Oh no, thought Callan, not that one, but sure enough it came. Komorowski hurled his drink at Callan's face and leaped for his gun hand. But if you know it's coming it's the easiest thing in the world to duck your head, and bring your knee up, and Callan did both. Komorowski went down moaning.

'You really do need a heavy,' Callan said. 'You're past it mate.'

Aunty Glad said waspishly, 'You'll need one yourself if you've got them Russians after you.'

'Maybe,' said Callan. 'But ask yourself one question, Miss de Courcy Mannering. How do you think I got this gun?'

The waspishness left her, and she looked down at Komorowski, moaning on the floor.

'You're scared,' said Callan. 'You've got a right to be. Now you do me a favour.'

'What?' she said.

'Ring the restaurant,' Callan said. 'Tell the head-waiter you're in conference and you don't want to be disturbed.'

She went to the phone.

Callan said, 'Do it right, Miss de Courcy Mannering.'

She did it right, and it was just as well. Callan had a lot of telephoning to do. But he didn't want them listening in on his conversation. He dragged the still moaning Komorowski to a cupboard, bundled Aunty Glad after him, and locked them both in.

The report of the second K.G.B. man's death reached Hunter just as he was about to leave for dinner at his club. He sent at once for Meres, and the messenger intercepted him just as he too was about to dine, and Meres resented it, but when he entered Hunter's office the old man seemed cheerful enough. At least he was pouring sherry, and that was usually a good sign.

'May I offer you some?' he asked. 'Or would you prefer to mix yourself one of those naval things?'

One of those naval things, Meres knew, meant pink gin of which he was fond, and of which Hunter disapproved. He chose sherry.

'Callan's just killed another one,' said Hunter.

'Good God,' said Meres. 'Without a gun?'

'He managed to get a gun,' Hunter said.

'I wouldn't have thought it was possible.'

'Nor would I,' said Hunter. 'It seems we underestimated his resources, his skill and his good fortune.'

'*Good* fortune, sir?'

'We'll come to that in a moment. He went to Palatine House. Do you know anything about it?'

'That ghastly monstrosity near the river? No sir, I'm afraid I don't.'

'Then you should,' said Hunter. 'Callan did a job there once. Not a big one, it's true, but it's on his file – and you were asked to make yourself familiar with his file, were you not?'

Suddenly Meres no longer felt hungry.

Hunter continued, genially enough: 'Palatine House contains, among other things, a rifle range. Somehow or other Callan lured the unfortunate Muscovite there and shot him – through the head and heart, I understand. With a high performance rifle that can't have been too difficult for him. Then he left the rifle and took the Muscovite's gun instead. Or so I should imagine. He was wearing a gun harness – but there wasn't a gun in it.'

'You mean to say those idiots there stored ammunition beside their rifles?' Meres asked.

'I do not,' said Hunter. 'The ammunition is stored elsewhere. The rules are very strict – and they are enforced.'

'I see what you mean about luck,' said Meres. 'Some idiot must have left a couple of rounds in the magazine. But of all the damn fool things to do–'

Hunter shook his head.

'There were no idiots,' he said. 'At least none in the rifle club. Callan must have provided the ammunition himself.'

'But that's impossible–'

Then Meres remembered going down to the armoury to bring Callan to Hunter. He'd been using a target pistol. A Woodsman was it?

'.22 ammunition,' said Hunter. 'High

270

velocity stuff. And Callan had two rounds – perhaps more. Where would he get them?' Meres made no answer. 'Only here, Toby.' Still Meres kept silent. 'And you searched him.'

'For a gun,' said Meres. 'I searched him for a gun.'

Hunter said, 'And now he's got one. I must hold you responsible for that.'

But there was no explosion, nor the least sign that one was imminent. Meres thought, He's so bloody glad Callan's got this far he can't even bear to bawl me out. It would spoil his mood.

'And then there was one,' said Hunter dreamily. 'And now Callan has a gun. The situation is piquant, don't you agree? We kept our bargain after all – apart from your regrettable oversight, an oversight which I trust you realise must never be mentioned.'

'Thank you sir,' said Meres.

'I read your report on Zhilkov, by the way,' Hunter said, 'and I accept your theory. The K.G.B. were on to him months ago.'

'He's given us almost nothing we can use,' said Meres.

'Ship him off somewhere,' Hunter said. 'A place in the sun and a pension. He brought us nothing, but we must not discourage the others. Let it be known that we're generous, Toby.'

'I'll see to it, sir.'

He finished his sherry and stood up, but Hunter wasn't quite ready to dismiss him.

'I wonder if Callan has got to Komorowski yet?' he said. 'And if he has – I wonder what he's going to do about him? And about you, Toby.'

18

Callan took a cab to the embankment. After all he could afford it, now that the K.G.B. was financing him – then walked to a pub and drank one more whisky. One more, he knew, wouldn't hurt him. But that was the limit until this lot was over. And that, more than likely, would be tonight. The last try, and probably the best one. Like the Old Guard at Waterloo. Callan hoped he could handle his problems the way Wellington had handled his. But then, of all the great captains, Wellington was unique in that he'd never lost a battle, and Callan knew already that there was one battle he couldn't win. The Scotch came, and he sipped it slowly, letting the delicate fire warm him. Christ he was tired: but there was still one to go. And after that – better phone his bird. It would be too bad if she was out when her warrior returned: if he returned.

'Hallo,' she said.

'You don't sound very happy.'

'I didn't know it was you,' she said.

'You still don't sound very happy.'

'I may be in trouble,' she said. 'Coloured people type trouble. Somebody seems to think my work permit's out of date, or something.'

'Can I come over and talk about it?'

'I told you,' she said. 'I told you last time you phoned. What makes you think there'll be a next time?'

'I'd like to talk about that too,' said Callan.

'In that case I'll get the rum out,' she said. 'Once you start to talk a girl doesn't have a chance.'

He left the phone booth and his coat banged against its door, metal thumped on wood. Two Gun Callan, he thought. On his way to the O.K. Corral. Two guns, and a knife you could slit faces with. And now he was off to fight the foe. Only the foe wouldn't be taking any chances, not now. He'd know about the man who fell into the caisson, and he'd know his other mate was missing at least, and even if that was all he knew, he wouldn't take any risks, not this time, because his orders were that Callan was to die, and he wouldn't be after any posthumous medals. Cover, ambush, a set-up where you could be sure your first shot would hit, a set-up where there'd be time for a second shot if the first one only disabled... A silencer? If he had to. But silencers were dodgy. No pro liked them. Better if he could find a place where noise didn't matter. Like a building site. But they'd used that gag once. They wouldn't try it again. And anyway, where this one was waiting, there weren't any building sites – just streets – houses and shops – and one factory. A factory that made metal boxes. Lorries coming and going, sheet metal dumped, clanging on to the ground, hand-hammers and rivet hammers and welding arcs that cracked like gun fire. The place was on a corner, and backed on to the river, and next to it was a bunch of derelict buildings; poor bastards driven out because they couldn't stand the noise. You'd never hear a revolver shot in that din: hell, you'd have to strain your ears to hear a point five machine gun. I bet that factory's still working a night shift, Callan thought, otherwise Ivan won't make his try. But with all that noise, and derelict buildings for cover, he'll be there all right. The mate he drew the sketch map for won't be there to help him, but he'll be there. He's too scared of his bosses to be anywhere else...

Long before he reached it, he knew that the factory was still working a night shift, but even so he moved in warily, watchful for ambush in the empty streets. But there was no cover for a man with Ivan's instructions, not unless Ivan was prepared to take enormous risks when he didn't have to – and Ivan would much prefer to take no risks at all. He was a pro. Callan worked his way from pool to pool of shadow, to where he could see the factory. Hearing was no problem at all.

From where he stood he was looking at the back of the building; the lorries delivered and left by a road that came up by the river. And that made it even better. There was even more noise than was needed – and no witnesses. They were all too busy inside, making noise. His eyes moved to the derelict buildings. The street lamps weren't too good, but the factory, was brilliantly lit, and the light poured out from its windows so that the houses near it showed clearly enough. But Ivan wouldn't be in one of them – it would be giving Callan too much of a chance. He strained his eyes to stare at the ruins, windows long since smashed, doors carted off for firewood.

Then he looked at the houses further from the factory, the ones that only the street lights reached. Dimness interspersed with darkness. That was where Ivan had to be. But this time there was no Lonely to act as a decoy and flush him out: this time the only decoy was himself... It would have been so easy just to walk away, to live to fight another day. But the trouble was that day would dawn, and there would be more fighting, no question of it, and Ivan would still be in the entrenched position, with Callan taking the risks ... or maybe not quite all of them. There was one old mate he could turn to: a strapping young feller who'd he glad to help him out. Carefully he moved back into the shadows, and found a phone.

Meres said, 'You must be mad.'

'I'm getting mad,' said Callan.

'But you can't possibly expect–'

'All I want you to do is help me shift a corpse,' said Callan. And that was true too – except he hadn't produced the corpse yet. 'Now, are you going to do it – or am I going to tell Hunter about the chat I had with Komorowski?'

Slowly, reluctantly, Meres said, 'Where are you?'

Callan told him. 'And don't stop to buy speed for your girlfriends,' he said.

Back then to the shadows and the waiting. If the killer was there, he would shortly have an edge – and if he wasn't then it was April Fool for Meres, and Callan would just disappear and leave him swearing. And meanwhile he waited, with the patience that was so much a part of his trade, moving silently from foot to foot, warming his hands so that they would be supple and quick when the time came. Suddenly he felt the first stab of pain behind his eyes. It came and went like a knife-thrust, but he knew it for what it was: a warning. Soon it would come back for longer and longer intervals; then it would be continuous, and the double vision would start. Come on, Meres, he thought. Move it you bastard. There isn't much time.

The car appeared at last, the big Lancia

Meres used for courting – and for shifting corpses. It moved with easy power to the ruined buildings, and Callan took the Smith and Wesson in his hand, crouched down like a sprinter, as Meres brought the car to a halt and got out, elegant as ever, his whole body stiff with outrage that he should be dragged to this abominable place, subjected to this vile and incessant noise. He moved towards the building, stumbling on broken brick. No doubt he was swearing, Callan thought, but he couldn't hear him – and then he did.

'Callan.' Meres roared. 'Callan! Where the hell are you?'

And that flushed Ivan out. It had to. He moved from behind a half-crumbled wall and put a gun on Meres. That meant he had to turn away from Callan, and that was about as much luck as Callan could expect, because to finish this one he had to get in closer, and this was his chance: most likely the only one. He kicked off and ran, crouching, towards the Lancia's bonnet, and for a second Ivan hesitated, uncertain whether to try for Callan or Meres, then swung the gun on Callan, and fired, as Meres dived into an open doorway. The bullet burned across Callan's left arm and he fired back as Ivan dived for cover, fired again, even as Ivan leaped, and knew he'd hit him, saw the ungainly flail of his leg as the man's leap took him behind a pile of slate and stone. Behind a car bonnet was no place to be, but it was the only cover there was – and Ivan wounded could be as dangerous as Ivan fit and well. Maybe even more so. If Ivan was going to die, he'd want company...

Another stab of pain, still quick, but longer than the last one. He had no time left at all. Callan breathed slowly and easily, then ran from the car, leaped for the shelter of an outside wall, and two shots slammed past him into the roadway. Ivan wanted company all right. Callan moved silently along the wall, closer and closer to the pile of slate and brick, then took off his coat, threw it gently forward so that it appeared at the edge of the wall. An arm and shoulder appeared, and two shots slammed into the coat, as Callan put one into the shoulder, then gathered himself for the last run that took him behind the pile of rubble, looking down at a man who was trying to pick up a pistol left-handed.

'Do svidanye,' said Callan, and the man reached out for the pistol again. Callan's foot came down on the hand and he groaned, then Callan picked up the pistol, and the man lay still.

So now it's three guns, Callan thought. And Hunter said I couldn't have one.

'All right, Toby,' he called. 'You can come out now.'

Warily Meres emerged from the house, looked down at Ivan. 'Well,' he said, 'aren't

279

you going to finish him?'

Callan shook his head.

'You can't let him live,' Meres said, then as Callan stayed silent, 'You can't expect me to do it for you either. Hunter gave us our orders.' Then at last in exasperation, 'Don't be so bloody squeamish. Finish him.'

Callan said, 'He is finished. Look at his leg.'

Meres crouched down and looked. A dark stain pulsed and spread down the man's trouser leg. 'Artery,' said Meres. 'Must have been your first shot. It looks as if you're luck's turned, Callan.'

Callan crouched down beside the Russian.

'You're dying,' he said. 'There's nothing we can do about it, even if we would.' There was no answer. The blood spurted rhythmically into a bright, sticky pool. 'You can't expect me to say I'm sorry I killed you – and I'm not. But I'm sorry about one thing – this whole stupid bloody mess.' The Russian closed his eyes. 'You were good, all right,' Callan said. 'My friend here's right. I was lucky.'

Meres bent down, touched the Russian's wrist. 'He's dead,' he said, then rose to his feet; his face transformed with rage.

'You bastard,' he said. 'I'll kill you for this.'

Callan lifted the magnum. 'I don't think you'll do it tonight,' he said.

Meres looked at the gun.

'You'd really use that?' he asked.

'I don't know,' said Callan. 'Let's find out.'

Meres looked just mad enough to try.

'But before we start,' said Callan, 'let's just remember one thing. You shopped me, Toby. You shopped me to the Ivans. You told them I was going blind.'

Meres looked at the gun: slowly the rage died.

'I'd like to know why,' Callan said.

'Hunter told me to make it as easy for them as possible,' said Meres.

'He didn't tell you to make it that easy,' said Callan. 'I have his word on it. We're supposed to be colleagues, Toby. Comrades in arms.'

Meres gave no answer.

'Is my job really that important to you?' said Callan. 'Because if it is you can have it.'

'You're lying,' said Meres. Callan shrugged. 'Once your eyes are cured – you'll never give up your job – any more than I will. It's all we're fit for, Callan.' He looked at the Russian.

'Do you really want me to move that?' he asked.

'No,' said Callan. 'You've done enough for one night. You can go.'

He waited by the body as Meres left, the engine revved and roared, one more noise in a battlefield of noise, then he turned away at last and followed the dark and lonely road to

281

the river. Three guns now: two Walther automatics, one Smith and Wesson Magnum revolver. One knife, single blade, K.G.B. for the use of. One detonator ditto. Callan, the walking arsenal. The river gleamed dully beside him. Throw them in, he thought. Get rid of them. Be an ordinary bloke going home to his ordinary bird. But it was too late for that. Much too late... The headache came back.

19

She opened the door as soon as he rang. She wore a dressing-gown of the same warm yellow as the rug on her floor. She looked beautiful: she always looked beautiful.

'Where have you been?' she said. 'I've been waiting for hours. The rum's getting cold.'

He moved inside, and closed the door behind him.

'Take your clothes off,' she said. 'Make yourself at home.'

Then she saw his arm, and the brittle, actressy voice changed at once.

'David,' she said. 'What happened?'

The room was as hot as the last time, and the heat was too much for him. He felt exhausted, and his head was banging like the bass drum in a Sousa march. He looked down at his arm. Coat and shirt were ripped apart, the skin beneath torn open, flesh bruised. He became aware that his arm was hurting, but not nearly as much as his head. Just a flesh wound, that was the line. Delivered nonchalantly, but with a brave yet tortured smile. He didn't use it.

'I burned it,' he said.

'That's a *burn?*'

'That's what they call it,' he said.

'Let me help you off with your coat.'

She did it neatly, efficiently, as she'd been taught, then rolled up the wreck of his shirt-sleeve, looked at his arm.

'It needs dressing,' she said. 'Just a minute.'

But weary or not he followed her to the bathroom, watched as she filled a bowl with water and disinfectant, then carried it back to the living-room. There were aspirin in the bathroom cabinet. He swallowed three, and put the bottle in his pocket. He was going to need it. Then she called out to him and he went to her, sat down and let her tend his arm. Her fingers were quite steady as she cleaned and dried the wound, fixed lint and bandage; but then they would be steady. It was what she'd been trained for. While she worked she said nothing, but when it was done she turned to him, almost frantic with the need to know.

'Well?' she said.

'I'd like a drink,' said Callan, and that too it seemed was medicinal. She went to the drinks trolley and brought him whisky, poured rum for herself.

'Can I make a phone call?' he said. 'Just one? Then I'll tell you.'

'It's that important?'

'I think so.'

She brought him the phone, then went out with the bowl. He dialled the number of

Lonely's home-from-home, and exchanged unpleasantries with the bloke who ran it, but he fetched Lonely at last.

'Mr Callan?'

'Yeah,' said Callan.

'Are you – all right?'

'I'm fine,' said Callan. –Apart from a splitting headache, and double vision about three minutes away, and an arm that's throbbing like a diesel. And other pain. 'Fine.'

'You fixed everything?' Lonely asked.

'Everything. Nobody's going to hurt you now.'

'Honest?'

The little man sounded incredulous. He had a right to be so.

Callan said solemnly, 'Cross my heart and hope to die.'

'You – attended to the other one?'

'All done,' said Callan. 'The firm's gone out of business.'

'Then I can leave here,' said Lonely.

'Of course.'

'Is it all right if I go to my Aunty Glad's?'

'I wouldn't advise it,' said Callan. 'She's a bit busy tonight.'

Lonely sighed. 'I got nowhere else I can go. Not where there's company.'

'Yes you have,' said Callan. 'Flat 3, Stanmore House, Duke William Street, Bayswater.'

'But that's your gaff.'

'Don't you want my company?'

'I'll be right over,' Lonely said.

'Give me an hour,' said Callan, 'then I'll see you.'

He hung up then, and she came back to the ting of the phone as it disconnected. 'Now perhaps you'll tell me,' she said.

'A man tried to kill me,' he said, 'but he wasn't that lucky.'

'You're not serious?'

'All that experience and you've never seen a gunshot wound?' he asked.

'No,' she said. 'This is my first.'

The pain stabbed deeper: he put his hand to his head.

'Your eyes,' she said. He nodded. 'I'll get the drops.'

She opened the cupboard and took out the small, flat packet, wrapped in its cellophane that the brown fingers tore open.

'You said you had trouble,' he said. 'Coloured immigrant type trouble.'

'My work permit,' she said. 'Somebody from the Department of Immigration rang my boss and said it was out of date.' She opened the box.

'And is it?'

'No. He was just being nosey. Lie back.'

'You never told me you love me,' said Callan. 'Do you?'

'That's for later,' she said. 'Lie back.'

Callan said, 'I want to hear you say it

286

before you put the drops in my eyes.'

'I–' she said. 'I–' Her hands began to shake.

He moved quickly, and the pain behind his eyes punished him, but his hand was too quick for hers even so, squeezing it half into a fist: the tiny ampoule in her palm.

'What happens if you break it?' said Callan. 'Do you lose your hand – or just your skin? Come on darling. Tell Whitey.'

His fingers squeezed harder, so that hers could now feel the glass of the ampoule.

'David,' she said. 'Please listen to me. Please.'

His fingers stopped then, still holding hers against the glass.

'I was the man from the Department of Immigration,' Callan said. 'I was very convincing – but then I used to be a Civil Servant myself – or didn't you know that? You had your job just three days before I came for treatment. You were far and away too well qualified for it, but it was the job you wanted – the only job you would take.'

'I like that kind of work,' she said. 'It gives me time for other things.'

'Like blinding me?'

'I wouldn't,' she said. 'I couldn't. Please David.'

'You were planted,' Callan said. 'Not to kill me – not if things worked out right – because you're new to this, aren't you? It's all a bit strange, sometimes. A bit unreal. Right?' But all her mind now was concerned with the glass under her fingers. All she could say was 'Please'.

'My guess is they first approached you in Barbados. Young and bright and beautiful and rich – and burning to put the world right. And when you lost your money – that made you even more their meat, because you signed on and they paid you – and I bet they got a receipt. Right?'

His hand tightened, and she said, 'David, please. It's going to break.'

'Right?'

She nodded her head and the fingers relaxed.

'So you set me up. David Callan – Super Mug. I even gave you my mate's address – not that they needed you to get it. That was just for openers–Your test piece as you might say. But once they saw you were reliable – they used you all right... You were perfect for them. I checked with you regularly. I had to. And when I checked in – I talked. And you passed it on.'

'You can prove all this?'

'I don't have to,' said Callan. 'We both know it's true. Just like we both know you spotted me as the blind man at the hospital – that morning you were late for work. You followed me in, didn't you darling? – And you saw the blind man was me. And you and I were the only ones who did know – until you

288

told the Ivans.'

'Ivans?'

'The Opposition, love. The Wet Job Boys. The K.G.B. They didn't teach you all that much, did they? But they taught you to pass on what you knew. And a lot of good it did them.'

'You're wrong,' she said. 'No matter what you do to me – they'll kill you.'

'They'll have a job,' said Callan. 'They're all dead. All three of them. I killed the last one on my way here – the one you phoned as soon as I told you I was coming over. You did phone him, didn't you, love?'

'Yes,' she said. 'I phoned him.'

His hand left hers, grabbed her wrist and twisted, and the ampoule fell to the floor. She tried to pull away, but the grip on her wrist was agonising; she couldn't move.

'I'll show you a trick,' said Callan. 'Watch.'

His shoe crunched down on the ampoule, and at once the bright yellow of the carpet rotted and withered to a dirty brown hole that crept slowly outwards.

'A great cure for headaches,' said Callan, and looked at her, bewildered. 'You went to bed with me. We made love. Or maybe you'd forgotten.'

'No,' she said. 'I hadn't forgotten.'

'Then why–?'

'I hate you,' she said. 'All you bloody Whiteys.'

289

'Except the Ivans?'

'Them too,' she said. 'Their system's fine and I love it. But not their colour. But you – you're infinitely worse than they are. You're the worst there is.'

'I killed them,' said Callan. 'They tried to kill me. That may not make me any better than they are – but it doesn't make me any worse.'

'Every time you kill you support your country's system,' she said. 'A system that's destroying my people. Just as you did in Malaya.'

'In Malaya a lot of Chinese tried to kill me,' said Callan.

'They were fighting for what was theirs. They had a right–'

'To kill me?'

'To kill anyone who exploited them; any exploiter, any colonialist. And that is what you are. Only you're worse than the others, because you're a better killer.'

'The Ivans told you this?'

'They told me everything about you.'

'You don't think they might have been a bit prejudiced?'

'No,' she said. 'I don't. I know all about men like you. A man like you killed Pete.'

'Pete?'

She looked at the sculpture.

'The man who made those.'

'So that's how he died.'

290

'Yes,' she said. 'That's how.'

'He was in this business?'

'He was a revolutionary,' she said. 'A good one. The kind who gets things done. And all the Whiteys were scared of him – so they sent for a man with a gun. A white man with a gun – and Pete died.'

'So you weren't worried about burning my eyes out?'

'I was worried about it,' she said. 'But I was prepared to do it– Or I thought I was.'

'You let me make love to you.'

'No,' she said. 'I didn't let you. We made love.'

'For God's sake,' said Callan.

She said patiently, as if she were explaining a very simple, very obvious fact: 'I'm in love with you – and I hate you.'

He released her hand. The pain behind his eyes was all part of the nightmare.

'That's why I drank so much,' she said. Then, 'I thought I would go crazy. I wish I had.'

Suddenly she reached out sideways, grabbing for her handbag, but Callan erupted from his chair and his whole body fell across hers, so that she cried out in a pain that echoed his. Still pinning her, he took the bag, opened it, and there was the last gun, a Bernadelli .22 automatic with a two inch barrel: six shot, non-projecting sight and only nine ounces in weight; just the gun for a lady – if the lady knew how to shoot... Her body moved beneath him, and her hands caressed his face. Beneath the robe he could feel the familiar, welcoming nakedness.

'You were always too clever for me Whitey,' she said.

He tried to pull away, but her arms came round him.

'Please stay awhile,' she said. 'You like it here. Remember?'

Callan said, 'I wish to God–' but her hand came up and caressed his mouth.

'Sh,' she said. 'You know God can't hear you.' She kissed him. 'We were good together. So good. But even that night you were too clever for me, weren't you?'

'You were supposed to call in the Ivans,' said Callan.

'Only I fell asleep first.'

He got up then, and put the Bernadelli in his pocket.

'I was going to die too,' she said. 'Do you believe me?'

'Yes,' he said. 'Get dressed.'

'Am I going somewhere?'

'To see a man called Hunter.'

'Your boss?'

'That's right.'

'Super Whitey,' she said.

She got up then, collected her clothes, then took off her robe. Her body was as perfect as he'd remembered, and she made no

292

move to hide it.

'I don't want you to forget me,' she said.

'I won't.'

She took a long time dressing, used lipstick and perfume, and examined herself critically at every stage. Slowly she became the woman he'd first met, elegant, proud, wary of white men.

'I'm ready,' she said. 'I'll just get my coat.'

Callan watched as she sought out a coat in her favourite yellow, belted it round her waist, pulled up the collar. Her hand trembled as it pulled the collar to her mouth, but he made no move to stop her.

'Goodbye Whitey,' she said, and bit into the cloth. She was dead before she reached the floor. He could smell a faint and pleasing odour of almonds, and there was a trickle of liquid down the side of her mouth. With that stuff it didn't take much, and it was as fast as a bullet. He put the gun back in her handbag, then knelt beside her and wiped her mouth, but that wasn't enough. She couldn't be left lying there on the floor like that; so he picked her up and laid her on the divan, and pulled down her skirts. Her body still portrayed that bounteous promise, but her face was that of a dead woman. It told him nothing at all... Then the double vision began.

293

20

He'd almost needed a gun to get a taxi, and the night nurse at the hospital had played hell and didn't want to let him go after he'd had the drops, but he'd got away at last and found another cab, and gone back home. As he climbed the stairs he realised how tired he was, and how alone. 'Goodbye Whitey.' It had been a very final goodbye, the only one that could free her from that terrible mixture of hate and love. He wondered for the thousandth time if she would have done what she'd been told to do – if she really would have put that stuff in his eyes? Her hands had shaken. She'd said, 'I was prepared to do it– Or I thought I was.' But she hadn't hesitated to go for the gun. She'd said, 'I was going to die too.'... Stop it Callan. It's finished. She's lying there in her warm, bright room, and she's dead.

He reached the door, and searched in his pocket for his keys. Then behind him Lonely's voice said, 'Mr Callan – tell her I'm a mate of yours.'

He turned round. Lonely stood in Miss Brewis's doorway, and facing him stood Miss Brewis. In her hand she held what appeared to be a bread knife, which was pointed, waveringly, at one part or another of Lonely's person. The niff was indescribable.

'I found this person at your door, Mr. Callan,' she said. 'He appeared to be trying to break in. And as you'd been away for some time–'

'You're very kind,' said Callan. 'But he is a friend of mine.'

Miss Brewis said distastefully, 'Then all I can say is that you have some very strange friends.'

'True enough,' said Callan. 'But he's not one of them.'

'Indeed?' Miss Brewis said. 'Then I hope I never meet the ones who are. Goodnight, Mr. Callan.' She turned to Lonely. 'As for you, if you intend to remain in the same room as any other human being, it is your Christian duty to take a bath before you do so.' Her door slammed.

'Blimey,' said Lonely.

Callan opened the door and they went inside.

'How come she didn't call the coppers?' Callan asked.

'Cos I told her you was on your way over to meet me,' said Lonely. 'You don't half have good locks on your door.'

'Why on earth didn't you just wait instead of trying them?'

'It's parky out there,' said Lonely. 'Anyway

you were late.'

'I'm sorry old son. I was held up.'

'Her and her bleeding bread knife,' Lonely said. 'Scared out of her knickers she was, but it didn't stop her jumping me. I'll never understand women, Mr. Callan.'

Callan said, 'Me neither.'

And then the phone rang.

He picked it up, and the voice said, 'Callan?'

Callan said, 'You've got the wrong number, love. This is the Home for Middle-Aged Orphans.'

'Charlie wants to speak to you,' she said, and Hunter came on at once.

'You've been the devil of a time getting back,' he said.

'I've been catching up with my love-life,' Callan said. 'It wasn't easy. I haven't got one.'

'I trust you're not drunk?'

'Not yet.'

'Then stay coherent till you get here.'

'I'm not coming to you.'

'Understandable I suppose,' said Hunter. 'I'll come to you.'

'Get lost Charlie.'

But Hunter had already hung up.

'Shall I make some tea?' Lonely asked.

'There's beer in the fridge,' said Callan, and looked round for the whisky.

'Look old son,' he said, 'I've got a – a feller coming to see me. Big feller. Runs a very tough mob. But don't worry – he's on my side.' Lonely relaxed. 'The only thing is, I think it would be better if you didn't see him.'

'Much better,' said Lonely. 'I'll drink in the kitchen.'

Carefully Callan unwrapped the parcel. First a bundle of money, his own, correct to a penny.

'You'll find your bank account's unfrozen too,' said Hunter.

Callan made no answer. Beneath the money was a box lined with cotton wool. In it were his soldiers.

'They haven't been damaged,' said Hunter.

Callan examined them one at a time. 'I like to be sure,' he said.

'I know you do,' said Hunter. 'That's why you're successful.'

The soldiers were unmarked.

'You forgot something,' Callan said, and poured more whisky. 'Two things.'

'A gun and a passport,' Hunter said. 'You can't have them. Not yet. Not till I'm rather more sure about you.'

'You'll never be totally sure about me ever again.'

'Why should I be,' said Hunter. 'You said you would kill me. Even so–'

'And one of these days I might,' said Callan. 'If you make an issue of it. I've got enough guns to do it, too.'

Hunter said patiently, 'I didn't come here to quarrel with you.'

'Just as well,' said Callan. 'I hate violence.'

Hunter sighed, and tried again.

'You've done very well, David,' he said. 'Very well indeed.'

'You're very kind,' said Callan, and poured more whisky.

'That was an objective statement of fact,' said Hunter. 'I've never been kind in my life. To kill four K.G.B. executives—'

'Three,' said Callan. 'The girl killed herself.'

'Yes,' said Hunter. 'Pity that. I would have enjoyed a little chat with her.' Callan drank. 'I'm afraid the K.G.B. haven't been quite honest over this.'

'How disappointing for you.'

'A lesson learned,' said Hunter. 'I shan't bargain with them again. When are you going to have your eyes attended to?'

'Couple of weeks.'

'So with any luck you should be fit in a month. You'll be on full pay of course—'

Callan poured more whisky.

'But not if you continue to drink at your present rate. Don't come back to me drunk.'

'I'm not coming back to you at all,' said Callan.

'Nonsense,' said Hunter. 'You bear me a grudge. I don't blame you. But you've had quite an adequate revenge.'

'Have I?'

'Indeed you have. To suggest to Scotland Yard that I show them my file on Komorowski–'

'Did you?'

'I was obliged to in the end. After a great deal of fuss. I dislike fuss.'

'Did they get him?'

'Not yet. But they're optimistic – I think with justification. Two warrants are out, as I understand it. Komorowski himself, and a Miss de Courcy Mannering – undoubtedly an alias.'

'Oh undoubtedly,' said Callan.

'Lonely's Aunty Glad,' said Hunter. 'You've had your revenge on all of us – including poor Toby. Now stop drinking and have your operation and come back where you belong.'

'You know something,' said Callan. 'I think you're in the stupidity business too.'

Hunter got into the Rolls and the car moved off at once. Beside him Meres waited, but the old man didn't seem in a hurry to speak.

'How was he sir?' Meres said at last.

'Callan? Drinking, but handling it well. But then he handles most things well. Wouldn't you say so?'

'He's good,' said Meres.

Hunter said, 'He's the best.'

'When is he coming back sir?'

'He says he isn't,' said Hunter, and remembered how Callan had talked about the West Indian negress. 'I wish that human emotion weren't such an enigma to me,' he said.

Meres ignored it.

'He isn't coming back?' he said.

'So he says.'

'Then he'll have to be taken care of.'

'By whom?' Hunter said waspishly. 'Do you feel competent to do it?' Then, deliberately, he relaxed. 'Forgive me, dear boy,' he said. 'I've had a trying day. And in any case the question doesn't arise. He'll be back soon enough.'

'You really think so sir?'

'Of course,' said Hunter. 'He's got nowhere else to go.'

Callan slept late, and woke to the smell of frying bacon. Tea was made, toast in the toaster, eggs sizzling in the pan.

'I think we're going to be very happy together,' he said. Lonely smirked.

'I got up early,' he said. 'Thought maybe you'd want to sleep on a bit. You didn't half put it away last night.'

'Drunk was I?'

'Paralytic,' said Lonely. 'Still, you put yourself to bed.' He turned an egg.

'Did I say anything stupid?'

'Fit to be loved, mostly,' said Lonely. 'I

don't know whether that's stupid or not.'

'Neither do I,' said Callan.

Lonely slid eggs and bacon on to a plate, took them to Callan.

'I put a phone call in a bit earlier like you told me,' he said. 'Bloke I know. He says he can get you a passport... Gun too if you want it.'

Callan looked at him.

'Just trying to make myself useful,' said Lonely.

Callan said, 'I know that, mate. Thanks. But I've got three guns already.'

'Blimey,' said Lonely. 'Maybe we ought to sell guns to him.'

Callan thought of Hunter, and the Stupidity Business, and the fact that he was never going back.

'Maybe one day,' he said, 'but not yet. Just now I think I'm going to need them.'

Boot.